Tender is the Brisket

STACIA FRIEDMAN

1

Mourners stood on a swatch of bright green Astro Turf, staring at a rosewood casket next to a pile of fresh New Jersey dirt. A rabbi who had never had the pleasure of knowing the deceased or his devoted wife and loving children extolled Sol Sheraton's virtues and spoke at length about his journey, as if Sol were on his way to a time-share in Martinique and not into a hole in the ground in Paramus.

Following the service, people streamed into the Sheratons' apartment in the El Coronado on Central Park West to pay their respects and to evaluate the market potential of the 3,000 square foot, four-bedroom, three-and-a-half bath residence with maid's room, working fireplace, built-in bookcases, updated kitchen, original crown moldings and stunning park views in a landmark building.

Ruth, who had arrived on the red-eye that morning, stood at a window overlooking the park, gazing down at trees brushed with ochre and sienna. In LA, where she had lived for over twenty years, spouses changed, agents changed, seasons stayed the same. Her eyes followed bright dots of color below, children racing around the same playground where she had once fallen off the jungle gym and chipped a tooth. She absentmindedly ran her tongue over the tooth, a flawless veneer, then turned her attention to the spread. Smoked fish platters from Barney Greengrass, a cheese plate from Zabar's. And the sweet table. It was enough to make her weep. Chocolate babka, cinnamon schnecken and miniature cheesecakes so tiny they could only give a stroke to Barbie.

Vaguely familiar strangers knocked back drinks and erupted into laughter. It was to be expected. Her father had lived a long life. The death certificate said congestive heart failure. Those who had worked with him at Sheraton Fashions, makers of fashion forward, plus-sized dresses, knew better. Sol Sheraton had died while getting a blow job from an Eighth Avenue hooker, a fate greatly admired by his peers. Ruth overheard this tantalizing detail while reaching for the whitefish salad. *Oh, Daddy!* She piled on raw onions and tomato.

People pressed cards into Ruth's hands. If there's anything I can do, they said. Realtors, financial planners, interior decorators. There was even an astrologist: Selma Rivkin, by appointment only.

"How you holding up?" asked a woman with deep-set, olive eyes.

It was her mother's younger sister Miri, her sleek cap of black hair now flecked with silver, her tawny skin a roadmap of too many winters in Boca.

"I'm good," Ruth said.

"And Nando?"

"Same as always."

Same lying, cheating, two-timing bastard. As far as her family knew, Nando was visiting relatives in Brazil. True enough. He had a wife and three children there.

"Your father was always so proud of you. We all are," Miri said, kissing Ruth, then wiping away the frosted coral smudge on her cheek.

Proud? I'm forty-two. Childless. Unemployed. Whoopee! Ruth's career as a television writer was considered glamorous the further away she was from the squat concrete building in Burbank that churned out the nation's nightly anesthetic of sitcoms. Back in L.A., television writers were accorded the same status as colonics practitioners. Marginally necessary, but not in demand at dinner parties. She had won an Emmy for *Pasadena,* a series drawn from her own dysfunctional family which was cancelled when the show's star got caught with a fifteen-year-old, a Dalmatian and a kilo of cocaine.

Then there was the age issue. Male writers continued to take meetings, pitch projects and get hired until they were on life support.

Female writers, on the other hand, were tossed out like sour milk after reaching the big Four Oh. Ruth's expiration date had passed. New York, a city where being middle-aged was only a misdemeanor, not a felony, held promise. Lately, Hollywood stars had been relocating to Manhattan in a movement so persistent it could be mistaken for Continental Drift. Alec Baldwin, Beyoncé, Sarah Jessica Parker, and now Ruth Sheraton whose star had diminished to a pen light.

Bolstered by a tall vodka with just enough cranberry juice to tint it pink, Ruth sat next to her sister on the sofa. Naomi kept her eyes on the embroidery in her lap, a swatch of linen stretched tightly across a circular wooden frame, giving the yarn a little tug to maintain tension. Naomi taught psychology at Meghilla University and wrote self-help books. Her latest, *The Highly Sensitive Person's Guide to Highly Insensitive People,* was flying off the shelves at WalMart. Ruth had always questioned Naomi's career path, stopping short of peering too closely into her own. *Say something nice.*

"What lovely needlepoint," Ruth said.

3

"It's not needlepoint," Naomi snapped. "It's crewel."

Ruth wanted to hug her sister but embraced her vodka instead. Naomi did not tolerate displays of affection. Ruth suspected her sister suffered from a form of Asperger's. High IQ and the social skills of a microwave. For her fiftieth birthday, Ruth had given Naomi a Donna Karan silk blouse with a price tag equal to the gross national product of Zimbabwe. Naomi hadn't acknowledged the gift, not a card, phone call or email. Typical.

Ruth felt like a spurned suitor. One who couldn't, wouldn't take the hint. But she's my *sister*, Ruth complained to her therapist. We're supposed to be best friends, right? At this point, her therapist would stroke her uni-brow, a luxuriant pelt that Frieda Khalo would've envied, and suggest they take this up at the *next* session.

As the baby of the family, Ruth could never quite shake the feeling that she had arrived at the end of the second act of her family's saga and, try as she might, she was doomed to flub her lines. There was so much Ruth wanted to say to Naomi. About missing Daddy. About coming home to start over. But where to begin? Instead, she took a deep, cleansing breath and went in search of her mother.

Ruth navigated her way through the crowd, down the hallway, peering into bedrooms, opening a door here. A door there. She caught a glimpse of Naomi's nineteen-year-old daughter, Shoshanna, giving mouth-to-mouth to a member of the catering staff. She opened another door. *Oops!* A man was pulling up his zipper in a bathroom. He looked just like Al Pacino. *Impossible.*

Ruth checked herself out in the hall mirror, her long pale face surrounded by a halo of auburn curls, her habitually sad eyes veering toward a mask of tragedy. Not a natural beauty

4

by a long shot. But Ruth knew how to work with what God and Lancome gave her.

She finally found her mother Dolly lying in bed, fully clothed, eyes open, a pile of bones swimming in a St. John suit. *Mom's shrinking.* Ruth climbed into the oceanic bed, wrapped her arms around her mother and planted kisses in her baby soft hair. Dolly had worn a page boy fluff with a dip over one eye as long as Ruth could remember. She had *good* hair, the kind that held a set from one salon visit to the next. For years, Dolly had it dyed a shade she called Diane Sawyer Blond. Recently, she had gone "natural," revealing a luminous platinum. Angel hair, Ruth thought.

"Whatsamatter, Mom?" Ruth asked, "Too many people?"

"Not enough people. Daddy's not here."

"At least you had fifty-four years of happiness."

"What are you talking about? Daddy slept with half the women here."

A dull hammer pounded in Ruth's head, tapping out a message she didn't want to hear.

"How come you never told me?" Ruth whispered.

"Told you what?"

"That you were unhappy."

"I was happy. I had my children. Your father had his whores. In my crowd, you don't leave a man for that. You leave a man if he doesn't provide. Your father provided plenty."

Ruth looked around the silk-swathed bedroom at her mother's collection of Daum crystal, closets filled with tasteful, tailored clothes, all in shades of beige. *Yes, Daddy had provided. But what about love?* Ruth felt a wave of pity for her mother. *How lonely she must've been all these years.*

"Sweetheart," Dolly said, "Tell me. Where is Daddy now?"

Ruth cringed.

"At Mount Lebanon Cemetery," she said.

"I know that. I mean, where *is* he?" Dolly turned to face her daughter. "On Friday, I was putting up a brisket, the way I do every Friday. Suddenly, there was this blinding white light in the kitchen. Like the ceiling was on fire. Then, just like that, it went dark. When I looked up, there was nothing there. A moment later, I got the call from the hospital. Daddy's dead. You see what I'm saying?"

"No, what?"

"The light. It was Daddy. Maybe he's still here somewhere."

Belief in an afterlife would've been helpful. But the Sheratons were a secular family, just a synagogue membership away from being devout atheists. Heaven was a Montauk beach house. Hell was the drive to get there.

"You miss him, huh?" Ruth said.

"Daddy took care of everything. How will I manage without him?"

"You could hire a financial planner or an accountant."

Dolly said something under her breath in Yiddish, then translated. "Never put yourself in the hands of a stranger."

To change the subject, Ruth told her mother about the man who looked like Al Pacino.

"Could be," Dolly said.

"Why would Al Pacino be here?"

"Your father liked to mix with theatre people."

"Well, there's someone else. I think she's a famous movie star."

"Show me."

Dolly got out of bed, slipped into her low-heeled Delmain pumps and accompanied Ruth to the crowded living room.

"Which one?" Dolly asked.

"Over there by the bookcase. The blond in the beige sweater with the mink collar."

"Yeh. She used to live in the building. Whatshername? Duncan? Dunlap? I don't know if she slept with your father but I always suspected."

"*Faye Dunaway* slept with Daddy?"

Dolly shrugged. She had taken a Valium and wasn't interested in details.

"What about that one?" Ruth tilted her head, "The tall woman with the pill box hat and the dark glasses? At the funeral she wore a full black veil."

"It's your brother Larry," Dolly said. "You should say hello."

Ruth had not seen her brother for twenty-five years, and when she had, he hadn't been wearing Givenchy.

2

Nothing had changed in Ruth's bedroom since she had left home at seventeen. Lavender walls and a purple shag rug that smelled faintly of pizza. French Provincial furniture from Macy's. A frilly canopy bed displaying a menagerie of ravaged stuffed animals. *Poor Snoopy.* A platoon of lipsticks, glitter eye shadows and a half-empty bottle of Anais Anais on a mirrored vanity. Looking down over it all, Bruce Springsteen glowered from a framed poster.

"Knock. Knock."

Larry stood in the doorway, pulling off a false eyelash. With his wig, makeup and high heels, her brother had been a passably attractive woman. In t-shirt and jeans, as he was now, Larry was a startlingly handsome man in his late forties. Tall, lanky, chiseled features, deep-set, haunting eyes.

"This isn't a good idea," he said. "You can't just drop in out of nowhere, without a plan and take advantage."

"And you can?" said Ruth.

"Mother invited me." He spoke with a crisp British accent. *Where did that come from?*

"Mother and I have always had a certain rapport," he said. "Now that she's alone, it seems the best solution for everyone."

"Since when does 'everyone' exclude me?"

"Oh, come on, Ruth. You and Mother never got along."

That's not true. We get along just fine as long as there's a continent between us. Ruth walked up to her brother and raised her hand. He flinched.

"Hold still," she ordered, reaching out to remove his other false eyelash.

"There. That's better," she said, standing nose to nose. "Listen Larry, give me some credit. You're the one who disappeared…"

"I didn't disappear. I was in Amsterdam. Mother had my address."

"I bet." *She probably cried all over her checkbook.*

Ruth stood close enough to smell her brother's cologne. Jean Paul Gautier. And something else. Fear. Larry had run off to Europe following a major fall-out with their father. Larry had wanted to go to Harvard Law. Daddy said fine. Larry had wanted to go to Harvard Law in plaid skirts and pearls. Daddy said over my dead body.

"How long are you staying?" Larry asked, arms crossed, foot tapping out Morse Code.

"Depends," she said, inspecting a sequined mini skirt, "How long are *you* staying?"

Ruth's tone was light, bordering on disinterest, but she felt an old, familiar, not entirely unpleasant tension between them, the kind that occurs only between siblings. The cord stretches and stretches, until one of them SNAPS. *It's not going to be me.*

"Children?" Their mother's thin, high voice, called from the kitchen.

Ruth and Larry made eye contact and drew a silent truce, reenacting a scene from their childhood. Whoever tells is a snitch. A tattletale. A *baby.* They filed into the kitchen with pasted-on expressions of congeniality. Dolly had apple cake on the kitchen table.

"As far as I'm concerned, you kids can stay forever," she said, pouring tea.

"But Mother," Larry interjected, "We need a plan. Ruth has boundary issues. If we don't establish a reasonable time frame for her to find an apartment, well, weeks could turn into months, years."

Christ. He hasn't changed. He still talks about me as if I'm not in the room.

"What's the problem?" Dolly said. "I have more rooms than I know what to do with."

"Yes, Larry. What's the problem?" Ruth echoed.

"The problem is…The problem is," he said, turning to his mother. "She upsets me."

"SHE? I'm right here, Larry," Ruth said.

"You see what I mean, Mother?" he whimpered. "She's so insensitive."

"She doesn't mean it, Sweetheart," said Dolly, cupping her son's face in her hands. "Ruthie loves you. Don't you Ruthie?"

I've got to get out of here before she opens her robe and breast feeds him.

* * * *

It was 3 a.m. Dolly couldn't sleep. She got out of bed and found her husband rummaging in the sub-Zero.

"What are you doing, Sol?" she said.

"What does it look like I'm doing?"

Dolly was puzzled. Not that her husband was in her kitchen rather than in his grave. But that he was wearing the robe with a large monogrammed "S." She was positive she had thrown it out. Sol had swiped it from a Sheraton Hotel. "They won't mind," he had said, "We're related." It was an old joke. Sol had changed his name from Shereshevsky to Sheraton soon after they were married. Better for business, he had reasoned.

"You want I should make some lox and eggs?" she asked.

"Don't bother. I'll just pick."

"I can heat up some kugel."

"Looks like you had some party," Sol said. "Who died?"

Dolly winced.

"Not a party, Sol. Just some friends and relatives."

He sat down at the kitchen table and ate coleslaw out of a Tupperware container.

"You look tired," Dolly said.

"And you, you look *gorgeous*."

Still with the flattery. No matter how far her husband's eyes wandered, and they had put on some serious mileage, they always came home to rest adoringly on her. *Gorgeous, he called her. After all these years.*

"Now that you're here, maybe I can get some sleep," Dolly said, giving Sol a kiss on top of his bald head.

He looked at her with a bemused expression.

"Sweetheart," he said, "Where else would I be?"

* * *

Ruth couldn't sleep either. Maybe just another sliver of apple cake.

"Mother? Who are you talking to?" said Ruth.

"Your father."

11

Ruth did not find this alarming. Amputees feel their missing limbs.

"How's he doing?" Ruth said, playing along.

"Good. Good," Dolly said.

Dolly turned back to Sol. *Where did he go?*

"C'mon, Mom," said Ruth. "Time to go to bed."

Ruth walked her mother to her bedroom, tucked her in and kissed her goodnight.

"Tomorrow, we'll all sit down and have dinner together. Daddy can't *wait* to see you," Dolly said.

In some realm, maybe it's true, Ruth thought. She wasn't religious, but she knew that her father's soul was now hovering between two worlds and, given the sordid circumstances of his death, if he were to make it to the other side, he would need all the help he could get.

3

Naomi awoke with a migraine. Not the dull hammering that pummeled her head once or twice a month, but a volcanic eruption of such magnitude she feared her skull would burst. It would do no good to complain to her husband. Howie slept in another room due to Naomi's snoring and believed that her migraines were psychosomatic. An excuse to avoid sex. Unable to stand, Naomi crawled out of bed on all fours to her personal shrine. Located on the east wall of her bedroom, the shrine consisted of a small bookcase draped with a sequined purple scarf, containing images torn from magazines, as well as dried herbs, sacred oils and a photo of Dr. Waldo Ramussen, founder of The Way.

"I deeply and completely accept myself," Naomi said, tapping her forehead, cheek, chin and breastbone. She had learned about Tapping, a method to quiet negative thoughts, from the Highly Sensitive Persons group to which she had belonged before she found The Way. Dr. Ramussen said it was okay to Tap and to do whatever enabled her to "progress." That was the key word. Progress.

Naomi had been making incredible progress. Really, she had. But then Daddy died and Ruth showed up, reawakening a torrent of voices inside her head: *Mommy doesn't love you. You'll never be as pretty and popular as Ruthie. You're STUPID.* Naomi recognized the voices. They were her own. None of her awards, honors or achievements squelched the nagging suspicion that she was no more than a grind who had doggedly climbed the academic ladder without so much as a flicker of brilliance.

"I deeply and completely accept myself," she chanted.

Before discovering The Way, Naomi had been just one more middle-aged Jewish woman with a PhD in psychology, a lackluster counseling job and a marriage held together by long silences and Lexapro. Thanks to Dr. Ramussen, Naomi was finally able to overcome her past, silence her negative loop and accept herself for what she really was. A genius. It made perfect sense. The most gifted among us are hidden, often from themselves, Ramussen said. The goal of The Way was to encourage gifted individuals such as Naomi to reveal themselves by creating abundance and sharing that abundance with – who else? - Dr. Ramussen.

After ten minutes of tapping, Naomi switched to the mantra of The Way. *I acknowledge the gifts which flow through my being of their own free will. There is nothing I need to do to attain these gifts or to release them. They are part of my being. No one can take these gifts away or alter them. I am a genius and that is okay.*

Although she hadn't written anything since her doctoral thesis, a dull, rambling work on ADD, Ramussen encouraged her to author a series of self-help books: *The Gifted Baby; The Gifted Child; The Gifted Adult.* The books sold well. (What mother didn't secretly believe her child was a genius?) The additional income didn't make Naomi rich, but it lifted her self-esteem and allowed her to indulge her daughter's demands.

The lava inside Naomi's head seemed to be cooling down. She stood with great effort. It was her knees again. The doctor had told her to lose fifty pounds or get knee replacements. Just thinking about it made her hungry. She shuffled into the kitchen, popped a cinnamon raisin bagel into the toaster and, while waiting, ate a slice of frozen strawberry cheesecake. Waste not, want not. She helped herself to a cup of Ethiopian roast Howard had thoughtfully left in the coffeemaker. Another thing the doctor wanted to take away. Caffeine. Impossible. It took two cups of coffee just to survive the subway ride from 97th Street to her office downtown.

Naomi was holding onto her counseling job until she made the best seller list, which was only a matter of time, according to Dr. Ramussen. Then her Gift would be revealed to the world and the world, in turn, would bestow upon her enormous wealth, fame and adoration. Naomi knew exactly what she would do with the money - move out of their cramped two-bedroom apartment where she and Howard had lived since he was in grad school. Her furniture would be butter-soft leather the color of pancake batter. With wall to wall white carpets and….her fantasy was interrupted by the phone. It was Shoshanna.

"Mother? I'm at Victoria's Secret and there's a problem with my credit card."

"What kind of problem, Sweetheart?"

"They say my account has been frozen."

Naomi's heart clenched. They had adopted Shoshanna as an infant from China, raised her as an Orthodox Jew and expected her to develop into a bright, well-mannered violinist or concert pianist. The only instrument Shoshanna ever mastered was her mother, whom she played like a virtuoso, biting, kicking, screaming, refusing to eat, causing Naomi to gaze enviously at other people's children. She'll

15

grow out of it, they said. And she did. The bossy behavior that had marked Shoshanna as the scourge of her pre-school was replaced by an ever increasing demand for designer labels her parents could ill afford and the lowest GPA in the history of Albert Einstein Talmud Torah for Girls. It's just a phase, Naomi told her husband. Fine, he said, but I'm not paying for it. To keep her husband happy, Naomi put a limit on her daughter's credit card. To keep her daughter happy, Naomi raised that limit every time Shoshanna's lower lip trembled.

"It must be a mistake," Naomi said. "I'll take care of it. Tell them to put your purchases on layaway and you can pick them up tomorrow."

"I will *not*," Shoshanna hissed. "Why are you embarrassing me?"

The lava started percolating again inside Naomi's head. Tears filled her eyes. She wanted to ask her daughter what in God's name she had to buy at Victoria's Secret that cost over five hundred dollars and could not wait another day. Was Shoshanna shipping hundreds of lacey thongs to refugees in Haiti? But Naomi knew from the metallic edge in her daughter's voice that this was not the time to discuss.

"Don't *ever* do this to me again," said Shoshanna, clicking off before Naomi could say I love you.

4

Larry strode into the bar at the St. Regis looking like he had stepped out of the cover of *GQ*. Lanvin suit, Ann Demeulemeester shirt and Berluti shoes. Admiring eyes, male and female, feasted on his dashing attire. It was almost as pleasurable as making an entrance in vintage Balenciaga, the supple fabrics gorgeously draping his long, lanky frame. He had spent the better part of the afternoon at Barney's. He scanned patrons, recognizing Tory's strawberry blond hair. She still wore it long, falling to her shoulders as when they were at Dalton.

"Larry! Oh, my gawd," Tory cried. "You haven't changed."

"Neither have you," he said, pecking her cheek and embracing a significantly fuller girth than the trim, athletic figure he remembered. But she wore it well, a single strand of pearls falling into the modest décolleté of a green silk blouse, her black skirt revealing muscular legs.

"Yeh, from the neck up," she grimaced. "But you, Jesus, what did you do? Thell your thoul to the Devil?"

Her lisp, which had been a source of embarrassment as a teenager, was somehow sexy now that tongue piercings were as common as lip gloss. Larry ordered a Red Snapper, the bar's signature Bloody Mary.

"Thorry you're here under such sad circumstances," Tory said.

"Actually, I was planning on coming back to New York regardless. This just pushed it up by a few weeks."

"Really?" Tory said, grabbing a handful of spiced almonds.

"If I can find the right *situation.*" Larry let that hang in the air a moment then squeezed Tory's arm. "Tell me what you've been up to?"

Tory's talked openly about her partnership in Manhattan's top firm, her short-lived marriage to a misogynistic corporate attorney and her weekend house in the Hamptons. None of it was news to Larry who had doggedly researched Tory's personal and professional life online, including her credit report.

"What good timing. We're both single," Larry said, clinking his glass against hers. She was the first girl he had kissed and vice versa. They had remained close through college and when they were both accepted at Harvard Law, they celebrated by drinking champagne at the Plaza and jumping fully clothed into the fountain. Their intimacy had never gone beyond furtive make-out sessions. Each suspected the other was gay.

"You never married?" Tory said.

"I never found the *right* one." Larry looked soulfully into her eyes.

"Me neither," she said, "This town is crawling with Mr. Wrongs." Not wanting to sound like a disgruntled contestant on *The Bachelor,* Tory asked, "What's with the British accent? I thought you were living in Amsterdam."

"Actually, I spent a lot of time in London."

"Really?"

"I went to law school there and worked for a firm that has offices in London and Amsterdam."

It was true, but with the kind of window dressing that came naturally to a man of Larry's temperament. After dropping out of Harvard, he had completed his law degree in Amsterdam, without passing the bar anywhere, and his only experience was pro bono work in Amsterdam's red light district.

"Really?" she said, rising to the bait.

He wished Tory would stop saying "really" but there were worse verbal ticks. The last woman he had lived with repeatedly chirped "Is that *so*?" like a demented parrot.

"Nothing exciting, I'm afraid," he said. "Just your usual. Custody battles. Restraining orders. Sexual discrimination."

Tory put down her fork and dabbed the corners of her mouth with the linen napkin.

"Sexual discrimination?"

"Mostly pro bono," he said dismissively. "You know, gender issues in the workplace."

Larry stopped short of explaining that the majority of his clients were employed in brothels and drag clubs.

"That's exactly the expertise we need," Tory said. "Transgender issues in the workplace, in colleges, high schools. Fuck. Even elementary schools. We can't keep up with the demand."

"Let's not ruin the evening with shop talk," Larry said. "I want to hear more about *you*. Still a whirling dervish on the tennis court?"

Tory tucked a loose strand of hair behind her ear and laughed, but Larry could see the wheels turning. He looked at his watch. Fifteen minutes to go. He leaned forward, his hand grazing hers ever so lightly, while she chattered away about tennis, her Pomeranians and fellow Dalton grads. At 6:29 p.m., he leaned back in his chair, pounded his fists on the table and said, "Christ. I'm starving. How about dinner?"

"Sure. There's a sushi place around the corner."

"Oh, I think we can do better," he said, flashing a killer smile.

Tory's eyeballs danced merrily as Larry guided her by the elbow into Ardour, the St. Regis' new Alaine Ducasse restaurant. If he hadn't extended an invitation, she would've gone home and washed down a Lean Cuisine with a glass of Chadonnay.

"Gawd," she murmured. "It's impossible to get a reservation here. You must know the secret word."

"As a matter of fact, I do."

The secret word had been a one hundred dollar handshake with the maitre'D.

* * * *

Larry dropped Tory off in front of her building on East 71st and instructed the taxi to take him to 90th and Central Park West. You get what you pay for, he mused, wallowing in the afterglow of a five-hundred-dollar dinner. His father would've jumped out of his casket if he had known. Sol loved making money but hated parting with it. He never understood Larry's need for season tickets to the ballet and opera at the tender age of fifteen. Or facials in college. That's what their big blowup had been about. Not Larry's penchant for wearing mini-skirts, but his kamikaze spending sprees.

"Money doesn't grow on trees," Sol would scream.

Oh, yes it does, Larry said to himself as the taxi careened through the park. He tipped the driver a ten on a twenty-five dollar fare and tap danced his way into the El Coronado. Tory had been super. Just as intelligent, good-humored and kind as he remembered. A bit butch, not a trace of lipstick or mascara and the beginning of a second chin, but that was no impediment to Larry's plan.

He danced into the apartment, executing spins and twirls. He flung off his Lanvin jacket, undid his tie and started a slow strip tease when he suddenly realized he wasn't alone.

"JESUS FUCKING CHRIST," he cried, a hand on his heart."What are *you* doing here?"

It was Ruth, stretched out on the sofa with *The Village Voice.*

"Um. Reading?"

"You said you were going back to LA today," he said.

"Did I?" she said, going back to the newspaper.

Larry stomped down the hall to his room, shutting his door with a loud thud.

"Sweet dreams," Ruth murmured.

5

$1,590, Spacious 1 bedroom sublet in beautiful Gramercy Park. Great Location! Great deal! Huge bedroom! Ruth was starting to think that apartment listings were crafted by the same wily con artists who wrote phone sex ads. It was an architecturally desirable, pre-war, doorman building on East 23rd. So far, so good. The apartment was on the twelfth floor. The hallway had sconce lighting, cream-colored walls, carpets devoid of stains. Ruth pressed the doorbell of 12-E.

"You must be Ruth," said a round-faced, smiling woman. "I'm Sippy."

Sippy wore an embroidered yarmulke perched on a military buzz-cut. Her short, rotund figure was camouflaged in a shapeless sweater, flowing skirt and combat boots.

"You're Jewish, right?" Sippy asked.

Ruth was taken aback. What did religion have to do with the sublet?

"We keep a kosher vegetarian home," Sippy explained.

"Oh, I see," said Ruth. But she didn't. Not yet.

The living room had a shit brown sofa, large flat screen TV and a plaid Barcolounger. *I could throw something over it. A circus tent.*

"Wait till you see the bedroom," Sippy said.

It was a 15' x 15' white box with a queen-sized bed, beige carpet and Ikea furniture. Humongous by New York standards. Sippy waited for a response, her plump hands clasped together in anticipation.

"Wow," Ruth said.

"I'm so glad you like it. How soon would you like to move in?"

"When are you leaving?"

Sippy's thick black brows knotted.

"Leaving?"

"I thought this was a sublet," said Ruth.

"It is. This is Batsheva's room. She's in Israel for the year. Maybe longer."

"Oh. So, you're looking for a roommate?"

Ruth had had roommates before. Some had turned into friends. Others had turned into material for her sit-coms. Ruth valued her privacy. She needed quiet in which to write. A roommate (or husband, for that matter) who lounged around all day or blasted the TV all night was as bad as living next to a meth lab.

"Are you here during the day?" Ruth asked.

"No. I'm a cantor at Congregation Either Or, the first synagogue in Manhattan to embrace the LGTB community. I'm also in a chorale group and do a lot of volunteer work."

The price is right. She seems nice enough.

Sippy held up both palms and waved them around Ruth's head as if she were shooing away flies.

"You have a pleasant aura," pronounced Sippy. You'll fit in well with the others."

"The others?"

"Five of us share this three-bedroom apartment. If you come back this evening you can meet my partner Beth and Chava and Simcha."

"I'm straight." Ruth blurted.

"That's okay," said Sippy.

"I don't keep kosher."

"We're not fanatics. As long as you don't bring beef or pork into the apartment."

Ruth pictured herself slumped on the recliner, fifty pounds heavier, dating a Talmudic scholar named Hepzibah. *If I need a bacon cheeseburger, I can go out.*

"So, where do you work?" Sippy asked.

"I'm unemployed just now," she said.

Ruth hadn't worked in over a year. As a television writer, she had learned to take the temperature of her career on a daily basis by checking the Neilson Ratings in *The Hollywood Reporter* or *Variety*. When her series was hot, everyone wanted to "do" lunch and discuss new projects. But when Trevor Monroe's off-screen escapades garnered higher ratings than the show, Ruth's career quickly went as cold as the seafood case at Whole Foods. Her name was no longer associated with a hit; it was associated with the industry's worst nightmare - an actor who believed he had built the pedestal upon which he stood. Production of the series stopped, while rumors flourished about who would replace Monroe. Johnny Depp? Hugh Grant?

Meanwhile, Ruth had collected unemployment and checked with Verizon to find out why her phone had stopped ringing. Her agent, Aloha Weinberg, said, "This too shall pass," and then stopped returning her calls. That was over a year ago and the mighty stream of unemployment checks and royalties had trickled down to an agonizing drip. Ruth had come to Manhattan with just enough money to cover a few months rent, but she was hopeful she'd wangle her way into a writing gig. If not a sitcom, then a soap. Same difference. Except the actors are in bed.

"What kind of work are you looking for?" said Sippy, licking her lips.

"Actually, I'm a television writer."

"Television writer, huh?"

"Look, I've taken up too much of your time," Ruth said, backing towards the door.

"No! Wait!"

Sippy flipped open her cell phone and exhibited impressive dexterity with her thumbs. Withdrawing a pen from voluminous folds of her sweater, she jotted down a name and number on the back of a flyer for a Women's Full Moon Circle.

"Debbie Sandler. She's the producer of *The Sid and Gabby Show.* Call her. Mention my name. Sippy Jacobs. We went to Camp Ramah together."

Ruth tucked the paper into her pocket, relieved to make her getaway, yet genuinely touched by Sippy's generosity. It had taken Ruth fifteen years to break into television in LA, which, in industry speak, meant the ability to get Powerful People on the phone. Ruth's contacts in LA were all on a first name basis. Chuck. Jerry. Hank. She attended their kids' bar mitzvahs, chatted with their wives at Pilates and commiserated with them at awards shows when they had to applaud enthusiastically for people they despised. In New York, Ruth had no juice. No buzz. Nada. Just a scrap of paper with the name of a woman who probably did not want to be reminded of things she had done with Sippy Jacobs at Camp Ramah.

6

The last apartment Ruth visited was in a building on West 83rd Street, between Columbus and Amsterdam. It was a narrow, four-story townhouse with yellow brickwork and black shutters. Ornamental wrought iron grates over the first floor and basement windows spoke of the neighborhood's past. She remembered cutting across 83rd as a teenager to get the Saint Agnes Branch of the New York Public Library. Cuban men sat on stoops on summer nights, slamming dominoes, drinking beer, the air sweetly scented with marijuana. Just around the corner, the stretch of Amsterdam Avenue formerly known as Murder Row was now spouting a fresh crop of Zagat-rated restaurants.

"It's a large studio. Second floor rear," the superintendent said. "The tenant is moving out the end of the month."

He had the saddest eyes she had ever seen. Ruth followed his jangling keys up the stairs. Garlic, onions and cilantro simmered behind a closed door somewhere. The hallways were clean and freshly painted a bright mango.

"You like it? I painted it a few days ago," he said.

He knocked on a door, waited, then used one of his keys. The first thing Ruth noticed was light streaming through tall bay windows. The walls were sand. The hardwood floors lacquered to a high gleam. A galley kitchen had the basics. The toilet flushed. The current tenant's décor wasn't Ruth's style. Too much chrome and glass. But those windows. They looked down over an enclosed courtyard. There was a round café table and two wooden chairs. Wisteria vines, now bare, snaked over a wooden trellis. Kale and golden mums bloomed in large clay pots. Ruth had almost forgotten the secret gardens of the Upper West Side, more coveted than roof decks or off-street parking.

"If you take the apartment, you can have access to the garden," he said.

"I can?"

"It belongs to the basement apartment but he's a cool guy." He smiled with his eyes, his teeth, his entire being. "I'm Alejandro Reyes. Call me Alex." He extended a warm firm hand. "You want to see the garden?"

Who says no to Michelangelo's *David?* Tousled hair, aquiline nose, pillowy lips, corded neck, eloquent hands. Still. Ruth hesitated, unsure where this would lead. The garden was connected to his apartment. His apartment had a bedroom. His bedroom had a bed. His bed…

"The garden?" he said.

"Oh. Sure."

She followed him downstairs. The delicious aroma was coming from his kitchen.

"Ropa vieja," said Alex.

His apartment was spotless and decidedly masculine. Black leather sofa and chairs, rough hewn wooden farm table, black and white photos of Central Park in snow on exposed brick walls. Floor to ceiling book shelves. A cowhide rug. The Marlboro Man could rest his spurs here. She followed him out to the garden. Water trickled in a small Zen fountain. Maple leaves from a neighbor's tree fluttered into the courtyard.

"I do my writing here," Alex said, removing his cap, combing his fingers through his hair.

A glorified janitor with literary aspirations was nothing new to Ruth. In LA everyone was a writer. A gynecologist had once pitched a screenplay between her spread knees.

"What kind of work do you do?" he asked.

There were times when Ruth dodged the subject, saying she was a dental hygienist, but not to a man with jungle eyes.

"I'm a writer too," she said.

"I thought so," he exclaimed. "Is that why you came back to New York? For a writing job?"

"No. My father died and I'm staying with my mother."

Shut up, Ruth. He didn't ask for the story of your life.

"Sorry to hear that," he said, placing a consoling hand on her arm.

He might as well have clamped a defibrillator on her. The surge was that powerful.

"So," he said, "What do you think?"

I think if you touch me again I'll rip your clothes off.

"The apartment? Do you want it?" he asked.

"Uh, how much is the rent?"

"Oh. Sorry," he said. "I talk to so many people. I thought I had told you. It's twenty-five hundred."

A month? For a studio? Alex read the disappointment on Ruth's face.

"If that's a problem, I can work something out with the landlord," he said. "Why don't you fill out an application anyway?"

He went into the kitchen and returned with two mugs of mint tea.

"How's it going?" he asked, sitting next to her.

28

"I'm afraid I don't look too good on paper."

"Let's see." He scanned the form, frowning. "Do you have any job prospects?"

"I'm talking to a producer at NBC."

It was a stretch. Ruth had yet to contact Debby Sandler.

Alex wrote NBC in the space marked Current Employer.

He gazed into her eyes. Their knees touched. A fire erupted between Ruth's legs. She looked down. There was puddle of hot tea in her lap.

7

Ruth found her mother in the den with a silver-haired man with watery blue eyes magnified by gold-rimmed glasses. The *Evening News* was on television, the volume muted, Brian Williams' lips moved silently. The man stood up and extended a brown speckled hand.

"Bernie Greenbaum. I was a friend of your father's."

And now my mother's. Ruth noted the dainty porcelain tea cups and chocolate babka. Her mother was using the Limoges. And wearing Chanel No. 5.

"Sit. Sit. Have some cake," Dolly said.

"No, thanks. I'm not hungry," Ruth lied, not wanting to make it a threesome. "But I'll join you for dinner later if you want company."

Dolly put her hand to her heart.

"What am I, an invalid? That you should sit with me when you can be out with *young people*? Besides, I won't be alone. Bernie's staying for dinner."

"If it's not too much trouble," he added.

"What trouble?" Dolly said.

Mr. Greenbaum smiled, revealing a substantial investment in cosmetic dentistry. Ruth went to her room, flung herself on the bed and wept. Daddy's cigars still clung to the walls and Mom was already warming up her brisket for another man.

8

"An apartment under three thousand dollars?" hooted Katya Romanov-Shmuckler, "I pay more than that for a parking space."

Arabesque, the impossibly beautiful restaurant Katya had selected, reminded Ruth of a Fragonard painting with its yellow silk walls, crystal chandeliers and patrons swathed in Prada, Chloe and Dior. *The recession must've ended while I was on the crosstown bus.*

"Where do poor people live?" asked Ruth.

"They commute." Katya looked out of the corner of her eye at the bus boy filling their water glasses.

Born in Moscow, Katya was employing a voice so deeply embellished with Slavic lament you could hear gypsy violins. Alternately, she could enunciate as clearly as a Chapin girl. They had met when they were both theater majors at N.Y.U. Back then, Ruth and Katya had a lot in common. Boys, yeast infections, the Future. After graduation, Ruth took off for LA and Katya tried her luck on off-off-off Broadway until she discovered the far brighter lights of serial marriage. Dr. Wesley Schmuckler, a Park Avenue plastic surgeon, was Katya's fourth or fifth husband, depending on whether she counted her starter marriage to a downwardly mobile actor.

"Don't tell me you gave up your adorable apartment in LA," said Katya, stabbing a leaf of radicchio, holding it in the vicinity of her mouth but not taking a bite.

Adorable was the term Katya used to describe things that were too small for her, be they apartments, diamonds or men.

"I had to," Ruth said.

"What did you do with all your furniture?"

Put it back where I found it. On the street.

"Sold it."

Ruth had placed all of her worldly possessions on the sidewalk, reenacting a ritual that was as indigenous to Santa Monica as a bikini wax. Strangers with foreign accents inspected her books, bounced on her Ikea sofa and haggled over price. Bit by bit, they carried off pieces of Ruth in rusted, uninsured cars. While Katya's standard of living had escalated, Ruth's had pitched forward and taken hair-pin turns. All they had in common now was the umbilical cord of the Past which wrapped itself around Ruth's neck in a strangle hold. Ruth wanted to celebrate her return to Manhattan. Katya was throwing a shroud over it.

"I don't understand why you can't live with your mother," said Katya.

"For the same reason I couldn't live with her when I was in college. She's a human doormat. My father walked all over her. Now it's Larry's turn. She never raises her voice. Never argues. You could pull out all her fingernails, one by one, and she'd apologize for not having a fresh manicure."

"But she's so sweet," Katya said.

"So is antifreeze." Ruth said. "If I stay there, I'll kill her. Or myself."

"Well, you can always stay with Max and me."

Impossible. The Katya of Ruth's college days had been a bohemian slob who thought Mr. Clean was a guy who showered before he screwed. But somewhere in her acquisition of husbands, Katya had become allergic to disorder. During lunch, she inspected cutlery and glassware for imaginary stains and complained bitterly about her housekeeper's dust-busting skills. Staying in her penthouse would be as relaxing as bedding down with the Marines in Kabul.

"I appreciate that but I have to get a place of my own," Ruth said. "I want to start over with a blank slate. Minimal furnishing. White walls. Hardwood floors. Neighbors who work the night shift and sleep all day. Total tranquility."

"That's not Manhattan, *dahrlink*. That's the Betty Ford Clinic," Katya said, raising her empty wine glass to capture the waiter's attention.

"The bottom line is that I have to find a place I can afford by the end of the month."

"You don't need an apartment. You need a man."

Ruth had given Katya the *Cliff Notes* version of her marital problems, implying that she and Nando were separated. *By 5,000 miles!* In Katya's world, when a marriage ended badly, the woman walked away with money, real estate and stock options. To be financially ruined by a man was gauche. Like wearing Versace with Uggs.

"This is going to be a challenge," said Katya, "But you have a lot going for you. You're new in town. You don't have children. And you're living in a fabulous building." She whipped out her Blackberry. "Ah. Here he is. Dewitt Clinton Hogworth."

9

When Dewitt "Witty" Hogworth called the next morning, Ruth was tempted to plead a headache. Dating took Energy and Hope, two commodities that were in short supply at the moment. It also took clothes. The vintage pajamas with high tops that she had worn to breakfast meetings in Malibu wouldn't cut it in Manhattan. Plus, the idea of addressing any man, other than Oscar Wilde, as Witty struck her as absurd.

"This isn't a good time," she said.

"I know. Katya told me."

Christ. What had that one-woman-Molotov Cocktail said?

"But if there's one thing I've learned about difficult times," Witty continued, "They pass more easily when you immerse yourself in art and beauty. There's a Matisse exhibition at MoMA I'd love to share with you. We can lunch at the Modern. I'll send my car."

His car? What the hell. A girl has to eat.

After trying on every scarf, belt and necklace her mothered owned, Ruth settled on a wide red lizard belt, circa 1970, with her black funeral dress. No earrings. No necklace. I'm in mourning, she thought.

When the silver Bentley pulled up in front of the El Coronado, the usually comatose concierge practically tripped over himself in a rush to open the door for Ruth. Cruising down Central Park West in a chauffeured car on a brilliant autumn day, she felt as giddy as if she were riding a float in the Macy's Parade. *What a gorgeous city! Why did I ever leave?*

The entrance to the Modern, the most pricey of all MoMA's restaurants, was as discrete as an after-hours club, no doubt for the explicit purpose of discouraging tourists from Topeka from mistaking it for a place where they could grab a burger.

"I'm meeting Dewitt Hogworth," Ruth told a hostess with chartreuse nails. It was at this late moment that it occurred to her that she had no idea what Witty looked like. Tall? Short? Slender? Obese? Katya hadn't provided a description other than the size of his investment portfolio. Vast. Ruth was led through a dimly lit bar to an adjoining dining room, a light-filled atrium with a view of the Rockefeller Sculpture Garden. Seated alone at what was undoubtedly the best table in the room, centrally located on a raised dais. Witty was detained. Would she care for an aperitif? Ruth ordered a white wine spritzer with lime. Something about this lunch date had the feeling of a command performance, one that happened with regularity and a familiar cast of players. *Is this what Witty did every Wednesday? Invite a different woman for lunch and had her served up, waiting at the table like an amusé-bouche?*

Ruth sipped her drink, settling into the opulent calm of the room. Perhaps Witty was right. What better cure for misery and grief than art and beauty? But what could a man who employed a uniformed chauffeur know of difficult times? Had he been forced to eat domestic caviar when the recession hit?

She looked forward to digging into Dewitt Hogworth's psyche with the zeal of a dentist prying into soft tissue. Her curiosity was strictly professional. The characters in Ruth's sit-coms did not spring entirely from her imagination; they were real people whom she altered with the playful abandon of a child assembling Mister Potato Head. This one's neurosis, that one's phobia, the end result being someone you instantly recognize, but aren't sure where you've met.

"Sorry to have kept you waiting," said Witty, leaning down to brush a smoothly shaven cheek against hers.

Dewitt "Witty" Hogworth was tall, trim and handsome in a silver-haired, Episcopalian sort of way. Over wine, Ruth learned that he had grown up in Darien, gone to Harvard and knew how to rig a jib. In other words, he wasn't Ruth's type. The men in her life tended to be financially unstable, moody artists given to political tirades and emotional meltdowns. There was the documentary filmmaker who spoke in whispers, another who made Art out of road kill and the poet who put her on the phone to resolve his issues with his ex. Nando had been the most normal of all. No artistic pretensions, other than his talent on the dance floor and in the sack.

"I haven't dated for awhile," Witty confided.

He spoke as if he had been far away, without ever clarifying where or why. *Rehab?*

"I try to maintain a balance, but you know how it is?" he said inhaling deeply and letting it out slowly. "Sometimes work is utterly consuming. That's why it's so important to come to this *sanctuary* and recharge."

Witty never fully explained his occupation but it seemed to have something to do with art and money. Lots of money.

A waiter recited the specials of the day, a soliloquy only a classically trained actor could deliver. Ruth longed for a menu without irony. Say, tuna on rye.

"I'll have the soup and a green salad," she said.

"And?" echoed the waiter.

"That's all," she said, handing him the menu.

Ruth wasn't watching her weight. Naturally slender with the metabolism of a chipmunk, she could eat whatever she wanted without gaining an ounce. Buttery croissants, hot fudge sundaes, pancakes with syrup, banana cream pie. However, when she was despondent, she couldn't eat. When Nando left, she lost ten pounds. Ruth didn't own Fat Pants. She owned Depressed Pants. Since her father's funeral, she had nibbled disinterestedly without partaking of an actual meal. Meals were for the living. Ruth was keeping company with the Dead. Witty didn't chide her, however, he restored the waiter's expectations of a tip by ordering zucchini blossom risotto with baby octopus, rare strip steak in basil emulsion and an eighty-dollar bottle of wine. When the food arrived, exquisitely plated, wondrously aromatic, bits and pieces found their way into Ruth's mouth while Witty distracted her with conversation, much the way a cunning parent tricks a toddler into eating peas.

"I envy your career," Witty said.

Uh oh. Here it comes. He will want to know if I've met Jennifer Aniston. She had. But that was not where Witty was headed. Dewitt Hogworth was a serious film buff. He spoke eloquently about the work of Visconti, Almovodar, Kar Wai Wong. Ruth was impressed. In her experience, men, especially those who carve castles out of stocks and bonds, had no patience for subtitles. They also tended to shun desserts under orders from their cardiologists. Men with money are in no hurry to die. But when the waiter combed invisible crumbs off the table and offered the dessert cart, Witty's face lit up like a five-year-old. Unable to make up his mind between a Chocolate Dacquoise, Lemon Napoleon or a Caramel Parfait, he ordered all three. This charmed Ruth and confirmed something she had suspected. Witty was gay. What other explanation was there for his ebullient personality, passion for the arts and single status? Ruth was not disappointed. She was relieved and dove into her dessert with abandon.

After lunch, Witty guided Ruth through the Matisse exhibition, commenting on the artist's brush strokes and use of light, pointing out Cubist influences.

"Did you study art in college?" Ruth asked.

"No. Art is a passion that came later in life."

Ruth waited for details that never came. *Did he collect prints, photographs, paintings? Was there a Rembrandt hanging over his bed?* Witty changed the subject, asking Ruth about her creative "process." She explained how writing, actually sitting down and putting words on paper, was part of it, but being curious, just watching people was equally important. Her eyes swept the room, taking in clusters of West Chester housewives with frosted hair, art students with pale sleepy faces and tourists conversing softly in French.

Witty asked Ruth a question. She didn't answer. She was distracted by a middle-aged couple who kissed, then wandered into the next gallery. Normally, Ruth smiled at displays of public affection. This time, she froze. The man was her brother-in-law, Howie Karp. And the sylph in the red sweater whom he kissed was not her sister Naomi.

10

"So, what's up?" Howie asked, tapping his Blackberry. He was a wiry guy who always looked, well, *wired.*

Ruth had asked him to meet her on the pretext of discussing a personal tax issue. They were in a rear booth at the Red Flame Coffeeshop, a half block from Howie's accounting firm.

"I'm not here to talk about taxes," Ruth said. "I'm here to talk about the woman you were with at MoMA yesterday."

"Jesus. People say the IRS is intrusive!" he seethed. "Are you following me?"

"I'm not following you. I was at the Museum with a friend and I saw you."

Howie shredded a paper napkin with his hands, tearing it into tiny bits, then rolling them up into balls.

"Okay," he said. "You saw me with another woman in a public place. Big deal."

"I saw you kiss her."

Howie puffed himself up and stared at her defiantly.

"What do you intend to do about it?" he hissed.

Ruth was flummoxed. She had expected remorse, regret, embarrassment, not antagonism.

"Well, I wanted to talk to you about it because….because…"

"Because you're a jealous little bitch and you can't wait to rub it into Naomi's face. You go off to Hollywood and you come back here and can't stand that your sister has a better life than you. She is a college professor *and* a published author."

A waitress plunked down Howie's "usual," pastrami on rye, and Ruth's BLT.

"I'm here because I care about Naomi," Ruth sputtered.

"Since *when*?" he sneered.

Ruth was seeing a side of her brother-in-law she hadn't glimpsed before. He wasn't just acerbic, he was mean.

"Look, Howie. I don't know how long this has been going on; I just don't want Naomi to get hurt."

"HAH!

"If we can't have a honest, intelligent conversation, I'm going to have to…"

"To what? Tell Naomi?"

"Well, yes…"

Howie noisily drained his Coke, grabbed the check and stood up. Then he leaned over, putting his face just inches from Ruth.

"You do what you gotta do," he snarled. "But if I hear one word about this from Naomi, I'm going to tell her that you invited me to lunch to seduce me and are pissed off because I rejected you. Who do you think she's going to believe?"

11

"Have you seen my pocketbook?" Dolly asked for the third time in twenty minutes.

"No, Mom," Ruth said "Are you going out?"

"No, but I *need* it."

Ruth found the missing handbag tucked snugly under Dolly's bedspread. She noted that there was precious little inside. An Estee Lauder lipstick in Coral Frost, a comb, a pack of Mentos and a few crumpled dollars. Dolly kept her valuables, including her credit cards in a "special place" which changed with such frequency that finding it was a treasure hunt that could take days. Once her pocketbook was located, Dolly sat on the sofa holding it on her lap as if waiting for a bus.

"If you're staying home, why do you need your bag, Mom?" Ruth said.

Dolly looked at her with alarm.

"Because I don't feel right without it."

Transference. Her mother had transferred her fierce attachment to her husband to a Coach handbag.

12

On the phone Debby Sandler had sounded large, dark and capable of breaking kneecaps. Ruth was surprised when a petite woman wearing over-sized, round, tortoise shell glasses extended her tiny hand.

"Thanks for coming in," Debby said.

Above Debby's desk, publicity shots of Sid and Gabby displayed frozen smiles and hair styles spanning four decades.

"Well, you know what we do here, right?" Debby lowered her voice to a conspiratorial tone. "I mean, Sid and Gabby have been around *forever*, so has their audience. Our biggest sponsor is Assure Adult Diapers."

Ruth shifted uncomfortably in her chair.

"We're all staffed up for now," Debby continued, "But Gabby could use some filler."

"Filler?"

"You know, the blah-blah-blah when the show starts and Gabby talks about what she did the previous night. Just two, three minutes of patter. Doesn't pay much. Five hundred a week."

"I'm interested."

"You are?" The disbelief in Debby's voice was palpable.

A young woman with magenta hair bounced into the room, saw Ruth and spun on her heels.

"It's okay, Vita, you can come in," Debby bellowed. "My assistant," she mouthed to Ruth with a roll of her eyes.

"It's for Melinda," Vita said, placing a large greeting card on the desk.

"Vita, this is Ruth Sheraton," said Debby, scrawling her signature on the card. "She will be replacing Melinda."

A cloud of confusion passed over Vita's face.

"Melinda's not coming back?"

"Not in the foreseeable future," Debby retorted.

It was a familiar moment to Ruth. Melinda was in detox or had found a job paying a living wage.

"So, will I actually be following Gabby around town?" Ruth asked.

Debby leaned forward.

"This is to go no further," she said. "Gabby Lee is agoraphobic. She *never* leaves her apartment. Every morning her driver has to practically pry her from her bed and carry her, kicking and screaming, to the limo."

"So, what I'm writing is…?"

"The fabulous life Gabby's fans want to hear about while they're having bagels and coffee and waiting for their first bowel movement of their day."

Ruth practically skipped up Fifth Avenue. Writing projects and deadlines were the pillars of her existence. Without them she was unmoored, adrift in her own personal Bermuda Triangle. So what if she was writing jokes for the Prune Juice Hour? It was W-O-R-K. She was alive again. As she was debating the merits of the free samples at the Lindt store – dark chocolate with pear or espresso - her phone rang. It was Larry.

"Mom's missing," he said.

13

Geneva, the Sheraton's housekeeper, was the first to notice Dolly's absence.

"Misses said she was going for a walk," Geneva repeated to each family member as they arrived, growing more hysterical with each retelling. "I thought nothing of it until *General Hospital* came on. Misses never misses her soaps. Never."

Larry questioned the doorman, then sprinted around the neighborhood, peering into the places a seventy-nine year old woman might wander. Coffee shops, bakeries, bodegas, delis. He found lots of elderly ladies hunched over cups of tea on a chilly October afternoon. None were Dolly.

"Has anyone tried the beauty salon at Saks?" asked Aunt Miri. "Maybe she switched her appointment?"

"That's the first place I called," said Geneva.

"Maybe she's visiting a neighbor?" suggested Naomi.

"I already thought of that," said Mr. Greenbaum. "I knocked on doors. No one's seen her."

Ruth sat beside him on the sofa.

"Thank you for being here," she said.

"Please," said Greenbaum, squeezing Ruth's hand. "Don't thank me. I've been through this. My wife..."

His eyes welled up. Greenbaum removed his glasses and pretended to clean them. Ruth kept her anxiety in check. Dolly had only been "missing" for three hours. Any moment she could walk through the door with her disarming smile and angel hair, surprised to find her living room filled with family and friends.

"I think we should notify the police," said Larry.

Geneva let out a long, keening wail.

"They won't take a missing person report until it's been twenty-four hours," Naomi interjected. Having volunteered at Meghilla University's Counseling Center, she had her share of hysterical calls from parents who hadn't heard from their darlings in four hours.

Miri signaled Ruth to the kitchen.

"Don't worry," Miri said, pulling Ruth into her embrace of cashmere and Diorissimo. "Everything's going to be alright."

Miri always knew what Ruth needed, often before Ruth was aware of it.

"Maybe she went to the cemetery," Ruth said.

"In Paramus?"

"She's been talking a lot about Daddy lately. Asking me where he is. She could've taken a taxi."

"That would be just like your mother." Miri said. "To run up a hundred dollar cab fare and ask some poor shmuck to wait while she looks for Sol."

Miri acted out Dolly picking her way among the graves.

"Sol? Sol? Where are you? I've brought you a nice brisket," Miri said, nailing Dolly's inflection.

When Miri laughed, her eyes smiled and the corners of her mouth turned down, a mask for comedy and tragedy.

"Stop. They'll hear us," Ruth said.

"So what?" said Miri dryly. "Did you see that wig on Larry? He looks like Mariah Carey on steroids."

Ruth howled, slapping Miri's arm. The phone rang. Ruth picked up the extension, doing her best to stifle her laughter.

"Hello?"

"Is this the Sheraton residence?"

"Yes."

"I'm calling from the Museum of Natural History…" said a perky young woman.

Great. They want a donation.

"I'm sorry, this isn't a good time…" Ruth said.

"We have your mother here…"

The Museum of Natural History was less than a ten minute walk from the El Coronado. Everyone wanted to join the rescue party.

"Ruth and I will go," Miri said. "Too many people will upset her."

Naomi, looking relieved, helped herself to a turkey sandwich with coleslaw and Russian dressing. Larry poured himself a glass of Chablis. Mr. Greenbaum shuffled back to his apartment and Geneva volubly thanked Jesus.

"Why would she go to the Museum?" Ruth asked as she and Miri speed-walked down Central Park West.

"I don't know," said Miri. "Maybe she went for a walk, got tired and wanted to sit down. Or use a restroom."

The Museum loomed before them, a maroon mastodon of a building. School buses were lined up on West 81st, collecting kids high on dinosaurs and sugary snacks. As a child, Ruth had been repulsed by the dead animals in their pointedly unnatural "natural" settings. The Museum's glassy-eyed inhabitants had terrified her. Going there now to collect her mother filled Ruth with dread. Suppose they had placed Dolly behind glass in her natural setting? Seated in

47

front of a muted television with graham crackers and tea, her handbag in her lap.

They found Dolly in the Security Office wearing her Bonnie Cashin caramel leather car coat and matching newsboy cap, an outfit bought in the 1960s that she still wore because "beautiful things never go out of style."

"Here they are," Dolly cried.

A guard pulled Ruth aside.

"We found her in North American Mammals. We figured she got separated from her family and made announcements on the loudspeaker. When no one responded, we asked to see her ID and contacted you."

"That's very kind of you," said Ruth.

"Not at all, ma'm. Happens every day," the guard said.

Miri and Ruth hailed a taxi even though it was only a few blocks back to the El Coronado.

"Why did you go to the Museum by yourself?" Ruth asked her mother.

"I wasn't by myself," Dolly said. "I was with my children."

14

One week later, Larry, Ruth and Naomi sat in the waiting room of Dr. Isaac Ziskin pretending to read *Yachting World, People* and *Glamour*. The speed at which Naomi had declared an emergency and rushed Mom to the doctor struck Ruth as a hysterical reaction to a normal occurrence. Dolly was almost eighty. What woman her age doesn't get a little confused? Especially a widow in the raw stage of mourning. Ruth had read Kubler Ross. She knew there was no normal when it came to bereavement. Dolly wasn't rending her clothes, wailing uncontrollably or beating her breasts. She got lost in the Museum. Big deal. Ruth had gotten lost in the Beverly Center.

"You can come in now," a nurse said.

They filed into the doctor's study. Ruth sat next to Dolly. Naomi sat at a distance, or as much as she could manage, moving her chair at an angle. Larry remained standing, hands on hips.

"Physically, Mother is in excellent health," said Ziskin, "I wanted you to be present while I ask her some standard questions to determine her cognitive function."

Dolly sat up straight, hands folded in her lap like a schoolgirl.

"What's today's date?" Ziskin asked her.

Dolly's smile faltered.

"Do you know what month it is?"

Ruth wanted to shout. *October. It's October.*

"Can you tell me what season of the year it is?" Ziskin asked.

Dolly looked out the window. The trees were in their autumn glory. She was wearing wool slacks, a cashmere sweater and leather coat.

"Summer?" she said.

More questions. Who is President? Where do you live? For Ruth, it was like watching her mother being stripped naked. And beaten. Dolly, however, seemed more amused than upset, giggling, as if this were a silly parlor game. Finally, Ziskin directed his remarks to Ruth, Larry and Naomi.

"Mother can no longer live alone," he announced, as if Dolly wasn't sitting right in front of him.

"I don't live alone," Dolly objected. "My children live with me."

Ziskin nodded and looked at Dolly sadly as if she were fading away before his eyes.

"This will be an adjustment for all of you," he said. "There are decisions to be made. I would like Mother to get a full neurological exam as soon as possible."

"I don't need an exam," Dolly said. "I feel fine."

Ziskin hadn't said the word but Ruth saw what he wrote on her mother's chart. Dementia. There had to be a mistake. How could that dreaded word possibly apply to the smartly dressed woman sitting beside her? The mother who always managed to keep a spotless home even with three children experimenting with chemistry sets, EZ-Bake ovens and

Magic Markers. Who set a beautiful table every night as if expecting Cary Grant and not a husband who belched and farted without apology.

Oh, Mom, this can't be happening. Not to you.

* * * *

Larry rushed off to a meeting. Naomi, to give a lecture on toxic parents. Ruth was left in charge of Dolly, a role that thrilled and terrified her. Here, at last, was a chance to prove that she was not the dreamy, capricious, irresponsible baby sister, incapable of caring for a house plant, let alone a demented mother. Ruth bundled Dolly into a cab and headed back to the El Coronado. The landscape flashing by was familiar but surreal because Ruth wasn't seeing it through her own eyes. She was seeing through her mother's. These trees. The bend in the road. The underpass. The crosstown bus. Did any of it make sense to her?

"How you doing, Mom?" Ruth asked, taking her mother's hand.

"I'm fine. But I want to get home." Dolly said. "You know you're father. When he walks in the door, dinner has to be on the table."

"Mom, Daddy's not coming home."

"What are you talking about? Of course, he's coming home."

"No, he's *not*. Daddy's dead."

"DEAD? My husband's DEAD?" Dolly wailed.

The cab driver whipped around in his seat. Oh, shit. *Why did I tell her? What was I thinking?*

"My god! My god!" Dolly's face crumbled in upon itself.

"It was over a month ago, Mom, remember?" Ruth said. "He had a heart attack at the factory? The funeral at Mt. Lebanon? The shiva?"

Waves of misery washed over Dolly's face.

"He's gone?" Dolly said, gulping back tears. "What will I do? What will I do?"

"Don't worry, Mom," Ruth said, drawing her mother close. "I'm here. I'll take care of you."

Ruth felt as if she had just discovered an abandoned infant on her doorstep. Helpless. Terrified. Inconsolable. I can do this, she thought. I, who never cared for a dog, a cat or a houseplant. I *can* do this.

15

There are times when seeing a Broadway show is ill advised. The day your dog dies. Your financial advisor eats a bullet. Or, in Ruth's case, you find out your mother has a degenerative neurological disease. So when Witty called and announced that he had snagged reservations at a new restaurant with a six-month waiting list and had fourth row center seats for *Kabul Serenade*, a musical comedy based loosely on the love life of General Petraeus, Ruth wanted to beg off with a migraine. She didn't have one. She had never had one. But now seemed a good time to start. She longed to climb into bed and stay there for, well, forever. Only one nagging thought motivated her to jam her feet into shoes designed by Torquemada and meet Witty in the lobby at five. Gabby Lee. The frothy patter Ruth had promised to deliver was not to be found by hiding inside her canopied bed.

"You look smashing," Witty said.

Ruth had worn the same little black dress, this time with a beaded sweater from her college days which made it "vintage." She felt almost stylish until she gazed at the female patrons at Shazam, a theater district restaurant where getting a reservation required the kind of clout associated with sleepovers in the Lincoln Bedroom. The problem wasn't that Ruth was over or under dressed. The problem was that she was dressed. Everywhere she looked, breasts popped out of bodices like playful pups straining at the leash. Witty, however, didn't seem to notice the undulating sea of female flesh. He was too busy conducting a Who's Who of the dining room. Yup. He's gay, Ruth thought.

"Don't look now," he said under his breath, "The woman in the leopard print dress is Lily St. Clair, the Bloomingdale's perfume girl who became known as the Madison Avenue Madame. She's with Zeitner, the ex-Congressman." Ruth had seen her that morning on the *Today Show* promoting her sexposé, *Tiger Lil.*

"He's living with her now, poor bastard," Witty said. "I don't know if that's irony or poetic justice."

"How so?"

"Well, he had it *all*. Money. Success. A devoted wife. Now what does he have? A woman half his age who's slept with most of the men in this room."

Ruth arched a questioning brow.

"Oh, not I," said Witty. "I don't enjoy the company of a woman who has her meter running."

Ruth smiled but wondered. What was the difference between the happy hooker at the next table and a woman like Katya who selected husbands on the thickness of their wallets?

Witty insisted on ordering champagne to celebrate Ruth's new job.

"I'm not on staff," she explained, "I'm just contributing bits of dialogue."

"Ah, so we'll just have a glass, not a whole bottle."

Once they were seated in the dining room, Witty ordered flutes of Dom Perignon."How's mother?" Witty asked.

Ruth had told him about Dolly's misadventure at the Museum but not about her diagnosis. The disease which must not be named.

"She's fine. She just gave us a scare."

Witty reached across the table and squeezed her hand.

"You look ravishing tonight," he said.

Ravishing? People still said that? Witty, by his own account, had been away from New York for a long time and had returned only a few months ago. From his arcane language, Ruth was beginning to suspect he had been on another planet. And yet, at that very moment, there was no one else with whom she would rather be. Dewitt Clinton Hogworth, with his Old School ways and gushing compliments, was exactly what Ruth needed. A big, puffy down comforter of optimism and money, to cushion the uncertainty that shook her awake at 3 a.m.

Pinot Grigio accompanied their seared scallop appetizer. A Cote du Rhone with the steak au poivre. Chocolate soufflé arrived with snifters of Grand Marnier; Ruth was happily tipsy. It only took one drink for her to achieve lift off. Two to rise above the clouds. And three to spiral into free fall. She excused herself to go to the ladies room, locked herself in a stall and laughed uncontrollably. All the tension of the past few days came bubbling to the surface. She wasn't laughing at Witty. She was laughing at herself. Laughing and peeing at the same time. Tears streaming down her face. She thought about all the hours she had spent in therapy talking, talking, talking. All the nights she had spent with Nando fighting, fighting, fighting. All the anti-depressants. The self-help books. The meditation courses she had taken and contortions she had twisted her body into to find the Holy Grail of well-being. And all the time the answer was a perfectly chilled flute of Dom Perignon, a juicy steak and the company of the kind of man she had avoided her entire life.

When she came out of the stall, Ruth felt reborn but her makeup looked as if it had been applied by a four-year old.

"You okay, honey?" asked the best-selling madam.

"Yes," said Ruth, wiping her eyes with a paper towel. "But I've ruined my makeup and I don't have anything but lipstick."

"Here, hon. I never leave home without it."

Lily St. Clair opened her metallic Gucci handbag, revealing enough cosmetics to stock Sephora. Ruth borrowed Bobbie Brown concealer, Smash Box eye liner, Dior mascara and Mac shadow. All in bolder shades than Ruth had ever dared. Lily's accent hinted at the not-so-mean streets of Scarsdale. Underneath her provocative attire and aggressive makeup, was the shadow of a young woman destined to marry a dentist and never leave Westchester County.

"Thank you so much," said Ruth.

"My pleasure," said Lily, dusting her face and cleavage with a copper bronzer.

"We working girls have to stick together."

Working? Do I look like a paid escort?

"That gentleman you're with is very attractive," Lily purred. "How long have you known him?"

Ruth was tempted to say "ten minutes," instead she told the truth as if Lily was a trusted friend and not the Whore of Babylon or, in this case, Bloomingdale's.

"He looks like a keeper," Lily winked.

* * * *

Paparazzi swarmed, blinding Ruth and Witty with their cameras as they entered the Eugene O'Neill Theatre. Ruth clung to Witty's arm, not out of affection as much as to avoid falling on her tush. Her heels and blood alcohol were higher than usual.

"They anybody?" asked a kid with a Nikon.

"Nay," said a guy with a telephoto lens the size of a surface-to-air missile.

The opening of *Kabul Serenade* attracted A-list celebrities because a Hollywood ingénue had been sprung from house arrest to play the lead. All the stars were there. Brad and Angelina, Jada and Will, Beyonce and Jay-Z. Although the storyline of an American army general brought down by a Tampa groupie had already been milked to death by late night talk shows, the dance number in infra-red with night-vision goggles brought down the house. By intermission, the makeup Ruth had carefully applied rolled down her cheeks from laughter. She didn't have to wait for the reviews in the *New York Times* to know what she was going to write for Gabby. Millions of viewers will pick up their phones and order tickets. I will make it happen, thought Ruth, warming up to the power inherent in being the hand that moves Gabby Lee's lips.

16

Sid: Hey, Gabby, what did you do last night?

Gabby: I tried out Shazam, that new restaurant on West 42nd Street. The food was orgasmic. If I was on Death Row and they asked me what I wanted for my last meal, I'd order their filet mignon in cognac and die with a smile on my face. For dessert, I had a chocolate soufflé that was so good, I licked my waiter.

And the ambience! The last time I saw that many mirrors was in Warren Beatty's bedroom. Everywhere I looked, I saw a fabulous celebrity – until I realized it was my own reflection. But seriously, it's a very happening place. I was sitting so close to a certain New York Congressman I was practically in his lap, but there was another woman there already. You know who I'm talking about - Lily St. Clair. The one who wrote that book, "Tiger Lily"? I don't care what anyone says. Ms. St. Clair is one classy broad. We met in the ladies room. I was having a mascara moment and Lily came to my rescue. (To camera) Lily, darling, *mi mascara es su mascara.*

Sid: What did you do after dinner?

Gabby: I saw the best musical comedy to hit Broadway in years. *Kabul Serenade.* It has everything. Fabulous dance numbers. Great songs. The set was incredible. I had no idea the Taliban could tap dance!

Sid: Any celebrity sightings?

Gabby: Are you kidding? There were more A-list actors in the audience than you'd see standing in line at Zabars on Sunday morning waiting for their quarter-pound of Nova. Angelina looked stunning in Versace. Beyoncé was ravishing in Ralph Lauren. She looked like she had been dipped in gold. I went up and thanked her personally for bringing a certain part of the female anatomy back in style.

Sunday morning, Ruth emailed the script to Debby Sandler. Minutes later, came the reply. "LOVE IT!" What a gig, Ruth thought, buttering her raisin toast. *I'm getting paid to have a good time and I don't have to sleep with anyone.* Last night, when Witty brought her to her door, he kissed her hand. Her hand, for Chrissake. But no sooner had she stretched out in bed with the Style section of the *Sunday Times* when there was a call from the front desk. Flowers for Ruth Sheraton. Tearing away the wrapping paper, she was dazzled by the fragrance and extravagance. White roses, orchids and hydrangea in a crystal vase. The card simply said, *Thank you for a lovely evening. Witty.*

* * * *

Ruth did not watch the shows she wrote. It was bad karma. Like watching your own sex videos. But on Monday morning, she turned on *The Sid and Gabby Show*. Wearing a plunging neckline that showed off more of Gabby Lee than anyone wanted to see at 10 a.m., the host chatted about the "fantabulous" time she had on Saturday night at Shazam and at the opening of *Kabul Serenade*. Gabby's timing was dead on. She knew exactly when to pause. Wait for a reaction. Or make a gesture. But Gabby didn't stick to the script. She called the Senator's companion "an all-day sucker." Made nasty comments about Brad and Angelina. Said their tongues were so deep in each other's mouths that by intermission Angelina was in her second trimester. The audience howled. Ruth turned off the television and called Debby Sandler.

"Deb. I just saw the show and I have some concerns."

"Shoot."

"Gabby went off-script" said Ruth. "Her remarks were mean-spirited. Libelous. This isn't what I do. I don't make jokes at other people's expense."

"Welcome to the world of Gabby Lee," said Debby. "Don't take it personal. She loves your work."

Click.

This wasn't the first time an actor rewrote Ruth's words with a pen dipped in smut. Staff writers was always "punching up" her *Pasadena* scripts with locker room language, causing sponsors to wince and ratings to skyrocket. "Never underestimate the audience's capacity for sleaze," said the show's producer, Bucky Marmelstein who went on to create the number one reality show *Who Wants to Be a Ho?*

I'm getting too old for this business, Ruth thought. The median age for television comedy writers was thirty. Young talent was welcomed as enthusiastically as virgins arriving at a frat house keg party. Older writers were tolerated, as long as they had recently garnered an Emmy and their last show hadn't tanked. But by the time a writer was over forty, the only way to get a seat at the table was to become a hyphenate, a producer-director, a level of command she had purposely avoided all these years. I don't want to be a bean counter, she told her agent. I don't want actors coming to me with their *ideas*. To this, Aloha would wave her hands as if drying her nail polish and sigh, "Don't say I didn't warn you."

17

"Where's Larry?" Naomi asked.

"In his room," said Dolly, clearly bewildered. *Who was this zoftig stranger?*

Naomi stomped, one could hardly call it a walk, down the hall and knocked on his bedroom door. No answer. Naomi could smell pot. She knocked again, then slowly opened the door. Larry was in bed, listening to his Ipod, smoking a joint, paperwork in piles all over the room. Upon seeing her, he jumped up and took a last long drag before stubbing out the joint. Naomi was allergic to pot but it was nice to see her brother in a button-down shirt and jeans. He was such a good-looking man, when he wanted to be.

"I can't breathe in here," she said.

"Ruth's out. We can work in the dining room."

Larry and Naomi carried armfuls of files to the dining room table, sat down and reviewed their mother's assets, safe from Ruth's prying eyes. It was what had always united them, a shared distrust of their sister, based on feelings so deeply buried in their psyches that neither could say what it was or when it had arisen. It was just something they *knew.* Ruth was their natural enemy. By the time she was born, Larry and Naomi had already divided up the Kingdom of Parental Love to their mutual satisfaction. The last thing they needed was a blue-eyed, curly-headed baby doll taking the spotlight. They did what any children threatened with abandonment would do. They tried to kill her.

When Naomi was four, she threw a heavy bronze bookend into Ruth's crib. Ruth screamed but she didn't die.

Not even close. Larry took a more scientific approach, holding the squealing infant upside down by her ankles and dropping her on her head on the nursery floor. Neither was successful, the baby lived, although there was a certain visceral pleasure in causing little Ruthie to howl. Mommy came running each time and, of course, by then, the guilty party was sitting quietly in a corner playing with toy ponies.

"Dad's money was all over the place," Larry said, handing Naomi a spread sheet. "Money markets, mutual funds, bonds, savings, checking, a couple of IRA's, real estate in Manhattan and Boca, and Sheraton Fashions. Basically, his investments were conservative, he did well."

"How much?" Naomi asked.

Larry enjoyed the moment. Naomi had no head for numbers. When she looked at a spread sheet all she saw were little black ants.

"Before we discuss money, we need to *position* ourselves for the long run," he said.

Naomi nodded and bit the cuticle of her thumb. Larry was always the planner. Naomi was his faithful assistant. She didn't realize until now how much she had missed him all these years, her handsome, charismatic brother who, unlike her husband, knew how to take charge.

"It will be best if all three of us sign on as Mother's power of attorney," he said.

At this, Naomi's thumb popped out of her mouth and her eyes grew wide with alarm.

"Hear me out," Larry continued. "If Ruth doesn't have power of attorney, she will start nosing around. But if we include her…" A smile animated his face. "If we include her, she'll be as liable as we are with one important difference."

Naomi leaned forward and licked her lips.

"She won't know where the money is," Larry said.

"And where is it?" Naomi asked.

"Right now, Chase Manhattan. But I'm going to, uh, move it around. We can start spending it down immediately, withdrawing a couple hundred a week. It's all perfectly legal."

"We can?" Naomi said, feeling the iceberg of Shoshanna's bills start to melt. "What about Ruth?"

"She doesn't need to know."

"But you said she'll share Power of Attorney."

Larry smiled mischievously. "That's the beauty of it. In theory, she'll have equal power over the estate. But, in reality, she won't have a clue."

Naomi licked her lips.

"What about Mother's will?" she asked.

"Patience. Patience," Larry said. "First, I have to find the most recent one. Then, I'll get to work on a new one."

"You can do that?"

"I'm a lawyer. I can do anything I want."

Dolly walked into the room, beaming, hands clasped, looking around expectantly.

"Oh, you didn't tell me you were having *company*," she said to Larry.

As soon as he heard his mother approach, Larry quickly turned over the documents and placed his arms on top of them.

"Are you going to introduce me to your friend?" Dolly asked.

Larry shot Naomi a meaningful glance.

"Mother, it's me, Naomi."

Dolly waved away the very idea. "My Naomi is a young girl, but I know you from somewhere. Do you live in the building?"

"I live on 110th Street with my husband Howie, Howie Karp."

"Howie Karp? The nebbish with a beard. My daughter used to go out with him."

"Right," said Naomi, hoping to steer her derailed mother back on track. "I *married* him."

"Better you than my Naomi. His beard reminded me of a *knish,*" Dolly said, using a Yiddish word with two meanings. A chopped liver pastry or female genitalia. In this case, Dolly was not comparing Howard Karp to an appetizer. With that, Dolly tottered back to her afternoon talk shows.

Passive aggressive, thought Naomi. As a teenager, she had resisted her mother's beautification attempts and adopted the downtown aesthetic. Unwashed, frizzy hair, black leotards and psychoanalysis. When she started therapy during her freshman year at Barnard, Naomi had a lot of anger toward her mother but didn't know why. Three years later, she knew. Mommy didn't love her *enough.* While taking courses on Jung, Naomi realized how intellectually and culturally superior she was to her mother. She read James Joyce. Mom read Jackie Collins. Even though she had her father's bulbous nose and her grandmother's double-wide hips, Naomi suspected she was adopted. What else could explain her innate intellectual superiority? So she asked her uneducated, ignorant parents to bankroll a year in Paris. Sol balked, but Dolly saw this as an opportunity for Naomi to attract a husband. Fat girls go abroad and come back svelte. Homely girls go abroad and come back with a certain *je ne sais quoi*. And brilliant, boring girls like Naomi come back, if not with husbands, then at least knowing how to wear a scarf.

So it came to pass. Standing in line at American Express in Paris, Naomi met Howie Karp and returned to New York sexually awakened and engaged to be wed. "What did I tell you?" Dolly prodded Sol. And yet. And yet for all of Naomi's accomplishments, she continued to feel she was the runner-up in her mother's affections. To assuage these feelings, there was only one cure. Revenge.

"Larry, there are several places that could take Mother immediately," Naomi said, digging in her purse and fanning out brochures from assisted living facilities and nursing homes. "It's for her own well-being."

18

"You can go back to L.A. now," Larry announced. "Mother is moving to Serenity Village in White Plains."

"WHAT? Why?" said Ruth, setting a Gristedes shopping bag on the kitchen table.

"Because she needs professional care. They have a dementia unit."

"A locked ward?"

"We can't have her wandering all over Manhattan."

"You're being premature," she said. "Mother is perfectly safe here."

"Ruth, be sensible. Geneva is only here three days a week and, frankly, I don't have time for this. Mother isn't going to get better. She's going to get worse. A lot worse. I put a deposit on the entry fee."

Never put yourself in the hands of a stranger. Ruth put away cans of soup, applesauce, graham crackers and ice cream, the new staples of her mother's diet. The doctor said to give her whatever she wanted. What she wanted was baby food. Ruth carried a small dish of butter pecan ice cream into the den where her mother was staring into her lap.

"Mom?"

Dolly looked up, the confusion in her eyes yielding to joy.

"Do you know how beautiful you are?" Dolly said.

It was the dementia speaking. Her mother's non-stop conversation had diminished to a few, highly-repeated phrases. Where's my handbag? When's Daddy coming home? Do you know how beautiful you are? It was a poignant question. Ruth did not have her mother's rose-petal skin, heart-shaped face, deep-set eyes, *shiksa* nose, Cupid's bowl lips and high cheek bones.

"When will I look like you?" she had asked her mother when she was thirteen.

Dolly didn't say "never." Instead, she marched Ruth into the lingerie department of Macy's and bought her a padded bra by Lily of France. Then she took her to Elizabeth Arden to have her kinky hair straightened. Dolly offered both her daughters a Kligman nose, so named for the surgeon that had taken a hammer to the face of every Jewish girl on the Upper West Side. Ruth accepted. Naomi declined. With Dolly's encouragement, Ruth blossomed into a tall, striking woman with an off-beat sense of fashion. When she moved to LA, she stopped subjecting her hair to chemicals and irons and her halo of red curls became her trademark, along with her penchant for accessories of a bygone era. Cocktail hats, Bakelite bangles and tortoise shell hand bags.

"Do you know how beautiful you are?" Dolly repeated, grasping Ruth's hand.

19

"Who died?" Dolly asked.

It was an appropriate question. The last time they were all together in one car had been for Sol's funeral.

"No one died," Ruth said. "We're going to look at a place for you."

"A place? I've got a beautiful place. What do I need with another one?"

They had been on the road for almost one hour. Larry drove his father's Lincoln Town Car. For the occasion, he had worn a sports jacket, button down shirt and jeans. Naomi sat next to him, poking a needle into her crewel work. Dolly was wedged between Ruth and Miri in the back. Ruth stared out the window at the Saw Mill Parkway. This is wrong. We're treating Mom like a child. A child who's going to overnight camp against her will. Except overnight camp is just for a few weeks and it doesn't have a locked ward. And why are we taking her so far away? Surely, there are excellent assisted living facilities in Manhattan. But Larry had been adamant. This is the *best* place, he insisted.

Ruth looked out the window at Bedford Hills and experienced a spasm of deja vu. She knew these storybook houses with white picket fences, the town green and pristine white clapboard library. Not from real life but from studio sound stages that duplicated small town America, where all hardships were resolved within the hour.

It was peaceful here. Idyllic. Maybe taking Mom out of Manhattan wasn't the worst idea. Ruth could see herself visiting her mother on weekends, poking around the little shops, having tea and scones in a café.

"Here we are," said Larry, turning into a long, winding driveway. A wooden sign planted in the lawn indicated they had arrived at Serenity Village. Moving slowly like a funeral procession, out of consideration for Dolly's shuffling gait, they made their way from the parking lot to the main building, a pseudo-Georgian manor with white pillars and dark green shutters. The foyer was a page ripped out of *House and Garden.* Schumaker wallpaper. Polished brass. Chippendale furniture. Fresh cut flowers. Off to the side, a fireplace glowed in a small parlor.

"You must be the Sheratons. Marge Pickett, admissions director," said a tall, bosomy woman with florid cheeks and a multitude of chins that disappeared into a floppy bow-tied, white polyester blouse.

If anyone doubted Ms. Pickett's title, it was engraved on a brass name tag pinned to the breast pocket of her margarine-colored blazer which coordinated with her plaid Pendleton skirt. And if anyone doubted her sincerity, Ms. Pickett spoke in the loud, hyper-enthusiastic voice of a woman used to making herself understood by the deaf. She leaned over and screamed at Dolly, "So nice to meet you."

Clasping large, glossy brochures to her chest, Marge Pickett led the Sheratons through the Community Room.

"This is where our residents spend most of their time," she said. "We have a full schedule of activities to keep them mentally and physically active. Plus, live entertainment on Sundays."

Two dozen bodies were slumped in chairs, eyes closed, mouths opened. If not for a black woman in purple hospital scrubs calling out bingo numbers, it could've been the City Morgue.

"This is our Media Room," sang Ms. Pickett, opening the door of another space filled with inert lumps of flesh. On the TV, a golf tournament in Pebble Beach panned out over the serpentine coastline.

"Here's the Dining Room," said Ms. Pickett. "It's a little early for lunch but why don't we sit down? I'll see if I can sneak something from the kitchen."

There were fresh flowers on every table. Starched linens. French windows looking out to a garden. Floral wallpaper. But something wasn't right. Ruth couldn't put her finger on it. Then, looking up at the Colonial light fixtures, it hit her. This *is* a stage set. Serenity Village had the artificiality of the Paramount back-lot. Ruth half expected stage hands to appear, snaking electric cords across the room.

Marge Pickett reappeared with a large plate of sugar cookies. A member of the kitchen staff in a long white apron with a blue paper bonnet on her head poured coffee and tea.

"What do you think so far?" Ms. Pickett hollered.

"Why is she yelling?" Dolly asked Ruth.

"Do you have residents who are highly sociable and ambulatory like my sister?" asked Miri.

"Good gracious, yes," hooted Ms. Pickett. "Right now they're on a trip to the mall. They should be back any minute. How 'bout you finish your coffee, then I'll show Mother her room?"

"My room?" asked Dolly, dunking a cookie in her coffee. "What kind of place is this?"

Everyone stared into their coffee.

"This is your new home," bellowed Ms. Pickett.

"The hell it is," said Dolly.

It was all downhill from there. Ms. Pickett developed a twitch in her left eye and smiled so hard she displayed her bridgework. Dolly clearly wanted no part of the tour. She wanted to go home.

"Is this a hospital?" she asked as they walked through a locked unit in which dazed women were still in bed at noon.

At Ms. Pickett's urging, Larry retrieved his mother's suitcase from the trunk of the car. Just then, the green and white Serenity Village van pulled into the driveway and unloaded a half dozen, ashen-faced old women. Some hobbled on walkers. Others were pushed by aides in wheelchairs. All had the glassy-eyed expression of prisoners looking forward to the highlight of their day. A hot bowl of tomato soup and Saltines.

"I'm going to take Mother to lunch," Ms. Pickette said, then silently mouthed, "You can go now."

Larry and Naomi speed-walked to the car. Miri followed. Ruth stared helplessly at her mother.

"Wait," cried Dolly, "Wait for me."

"Come on, Mrs. Sheraton," said Ms. Pickett, "Let's go to the dining room."

"Don't leave me here," Dolly wailed.

Ruth got as far as the door and stopped. One of her mother's Yiddish proverbs came back to her. *Never put yourself in the hands of a stranger.* She ran back, grabbed her mother's hand and the suitcase.

"Mother needs time to adjust." hissed Ms. Pickett.

"Don't tell me what my mother needs," said Ruth.

Larry was at the wheel with the motor running.

"What the hell's going on?" he said, turning around in his seat.

"We're going home," said Ruth, helping Dolly into the car.

"But I gave them a deposit," said Larry.

"You'll have to get it back," said Ruth.

"This is an excellent place," said Larry, bristling with exasperation. "They have an outstanding reputation. It's not going to be better anywhere else."

"Ruth, he has a point," Miri said gently, "If you don't like this place, you're not going to like any of them."

"This isn't about what I like or what you like," said Ruth. "It's about what Mom likes. It's her money and her life."

"That's right, dear," Dolly said, patting Ruth's hand.

Larry glared at Ruth through the rear view mirror.

"So what's the alternative?" he said.

"Mom can stay at the El Coronado," Ruth said.

"That's right, dear," Dolly repeated.

"And who is going to care for her 24/7?" asked Larry.

"*I* will," Ruth said, "I'll take care of her."

She recognized in her voice the shrill insistence of a five-year-old vowing to care for a pet turtle or parakeet, knowing if she failed, Dolly Sheraton could not be flushed down the toilet or coaxed out an open window. Ruth had lost so much in the last year. Her career. Her marriage. Her father. Dolly was all she had left and she wasn't about to let go.

20

Ruth pressed the door buzzer marked Superintendent, half hoping no one would answer. Just as she turned to leave, the door swung open.

"Hey," said Alex, sleepy-eyed and unshaven.

"Hi," she said, "Sorry to come by so early…"

"No problem. I was just having coffee."

Ruth followed Alex downstairs, through his apartment to the garden. The surrounding buildings provided shelter from the wind, causing the courtyard to feel warmer than the street. That was the logical explanation. However, Ruth was more inclined to believe that Alex radiated his own personal sub-tropical climate.

"How do you take your coffee?" he asked.

"Cream, no sugar. Thanks."

Moments later, he handed her a steaming mug. It smelled like espresso.

"Café Bustello," he said. "It fuels my writing."

Her eyes went to a notebook on the table. Loopy scrawl covered half the page.

"Sorry if I interrupted," she said. *Stop apologizing, Ruth.*

"No. No. I'm glad you came," he said. "I've been thinking about you."

"You have?" Her voice jumped an octave.

"Writing is so solitary. So isolating," he said. "All that time, rummaging around inside my own head. I'm looking forward to having you…..." His big Bambi eyes locked on hers. "Having you in the building."

"Well, actually…" Ruth poised herself for a swan dive. "I can't take the apartment."

"Why not?" He seemed genuinely crushed. "Is it the rent?"

"It's my mother. She's not doing well. If I don't take care of her my family is going to put her in one of those places."

"Oh, nooooo." groaned Alex, wrapping his long brown fingers around her hand. He was trying to console her but the effect of his flesh on hers was electrifying. "Of course, you must take care of your mother. I would do the same. Where does she live?"

"At the El Coronado…"

Alex's eyebrows rose ever so slightly. *Don't look at me like that. I'm not rich,* she wanted to scream. Everyone knew the building with its twin cupolas rising majestically over Central Park like gargantuan breast implants. Its name alone carried a certain cache. Money. Not old New York money but freshly-minted money that carried the scent of Brooklyn, Queens and, if you sniffed deeply, Minsk. When she was young and hanging out in the Village, Ruth told people she was from the Upper West side, but avoided mention of the El Coronado for fear she would not be taken seriously.

"My parents moved there from Flatbush before I was born," Ruth said, taking herself out of the equation and, hopefully, regaining Alex's respect.

"Come inside," he said, still holding her hand. "I want to show you something."

Ruth's mind raced. She allowed him to lead her into his apartment. Into his bedroom. *What am I doing? What's happening? Am I wearing matching undies today? Did I shave my legs?* Her heart raced in her ears. Alex removed a book from a shelf and handed it to her. *Mambo Nights* by Alejandro Reyes.

"It's my first publication, a collection of short stories," he said. "I know it's asking a lot but would you read it and give me your honest opinion?"

"Oh. Yes. I'd be happy to."

Ruth was relieved and disappointed. Of all the things a man could ask of a woman in a bedroom, Alex wanted a literary critique. It was just as well. She remembered she was wearing a sports bra and Hanes underpants.

* * * *

"Are you fucking nuts?" Katya said, lifting her Yorkiepoo out of her Ferragamo bag and putting him on the pavement.

"What can assisted living do for her that I can't do?" Ruth countered.

"They have an entire staff," Katya said. "You're just one person. Besides, your mother isn't your mother anymore. She's already *gone*."

It was a remark Ruth heard before and it made her furious.

"She's lost her memory. Not her mind," she stammered.

"Okay. Okay." Katya wagging her head in surrender. "But the last time I suggested you live with her, you went ballistic."

Ruth, who had made a career out of putting words in other people's mouths, was at a loss to explain the seismic shift in her relationship with her mother. For as long as Ruth could remember, conversations with Dolly had always ended

76

in recriminations and tears. Shopping trips turned into shouting matches. Don't let Daddy push you around, Ruth would say. Stand up for yourself, she'd say. Alright, dear, I've got to go home now and put dinner on the table for your father, Dolly would say.

Ruth was forever mining the elusive vein of anger in her mother's façade of acquiescence. It had to be there. No one is born to serve brisket in silence. It wasn't her father's death, the stigmata of widowhood, that caused Ruth to declare a truce. It was the dementia. All her life, Ruth had despised Dolly's vulnerability and now, here she was, dedicating herself to protecting it.

"I'm not losing my freedom," Ruth said, "I'm gaining a rent-free apartment."

"Well, just so this isn't about Who Does Mommy Love Best?"

"Fuck no," Ruth snorted.

"Because if it is, you're going to be very disappointed."

Katya had once toyed with the idea of becoming a therapist just long enough to leaf through a New School catalogue, but had decided that listening to other people's problems was bad karma.

"So you're not taking the studio on West 83rd ?" Katya continued.

"Can't afford it."

"What about the hottie who lives in the basement?"

"I can't afford him either," Ruth sighed. "He's Latino like Nando. Probably hits on every woman who walks in the place. "

The dog was madly sniffing the base of a maple tree.

"C'mon, Pushkin," Katya said. "Make *caca* for Mommy."

While Pushkin squatted, Katya got out a Wetnap.

"You're over-thinking things," Katya said. "Who cares what he does with other women? You could use a little *divertissement.*"

Ah, Ruth thought, so she knows Witty is gay. Katya wiped Pushkin's fluffy little ass, then tucked him back in her handbag.

"Aren't you going to pick that up?" Ruth said, indicating the tiny turds on the ground.

"Don't be ridiculous. It would be like picking up after a squirrel."

Katya linked her arm in Ruth's as they continued window shopping, gazing at designer duds Ruth couldn't possibly afford. Chanel, Krizia, Gianfranco Ferre.

"I have one just like that," Ruth said, pointing at a studded black leather mini skirt. "But I didn't pay two thousand for it. I got it at a resale shop for fifty bucks."

"How's it going with Witty?" said Katya, while her dog lapped her face.

"Okay, I guess," Ruth said without enthusiasm. "Every week he takes me to another art opening or a Broadway show."

Witty was as dependable as the Uptown Express, albeit with more elegant trappings. He arrived punctually at the El Coronado every Saturday evening, immaculately groomed, armed with roses, chocolates, theatre tickets and restaurant reservations, while his chauffeur-driven, silver Bentley purred on Central Park West. Ruth raided her mother's closet, then her brother's before making the rounds of

Eastside consignment shops to keep up appearances. And yet, she was just going through the motions. While she grazed on foie gras and nestled in the buttery leather of Witty's Bentley, all she could think of was Alex.

"Well, what more do you want, *dahlink*? You've only known Witty a short time. You can't expect him to take you to Paris for the weekend. Although, if you play your cards right, that may happen soon enough."

Ruth stopped walking.

"I don't want to go to Paris with Witty. He's a nice guy but there's no, no chemistry."

"Chemistry?" Katya snorted, steering Ruth to a back table at Maison du Chocolat. Over mugs of hot chocolate as thick as pudding, Katya revealed how she balanced her married life to a workaholic surgeon with her need for passion and romance.

"A woman has needs and wants," Katya said, "Husbands provide the needs, lovers fulfill the wants. It's a perfect system, if you don't break the rules."

"Rules?" Ruth yelped. "What about thou shalt not?"

"You're innocence is charming but it's outdated," Katya said. "Adultery is only destructive if it leads to divorce and it doesn't unless you're careless. If you're lucky enough to snag a big tuna like Dewitt Hogworth, you don't screw around with men in the same pond. You have your little *matinees* with your Latino hottie. But be discrete. You know what they say. Loose hips sink ships."

Ruth did not correct her. Katya's malapropisms did not spring from ignorance of the English language. They came from the love of it.

"And you do not, I repeat, you do *not* fall in love with him," Katya intoned, applying lip gloss as viscous as honey.

When they air-kissed and parted on the corner of 80th and Madison, each woman felt morally superior to the other. How can she live without love, Ruth wondered. How can she live without money, Katya shuddered, then circled back to buy the leather mini skirt.

21

"Are you sleeping?" Sol asked.

Dolly snored voluptuously by way of reply.

Sol inched closer, working his hand under her nightgown, pinching her nipple.

"Dolllllllleeee," he sang softly into her ear.

"I'm sleeping," she snorted, pushing his hand away and turning her back.

"No, you're not," he said, spooning her into his furry belly.

This time his hand inched its way down, down, down between her legs. His penis prodded her from behind, as hard and insistent as when he was a young buck.

"STOP THAT!" Dolly said, pulling herself into a sitting position and turning on the lamp. She had been dreaming about her first sweetheart. They were going to elope. And now here she was in bed with whatshisname.

Sol pulled his wounded Basset Hound face. All innocence and pain.

"Have some respect," Dolly snapped. "A woman my age needs her sleep."

"Your age?" Sol said in bewilderment. "You're in the prime of life."

"Yeh, and apples are still ten cents a pound."

"For God's sake. Look in the mirror."

He took her by the hand to the full length mirror. Dolly couldn't believe her eyes. There wasn't a line on her face.

Her skin was as smooth, and her hair was the Titian blonde of her childhood. Sol had wavy, black hair, a lithe body and an erection pointing to the ceiling.

"I *am* young," she gasped.

"And beautiful," Sol said, sliding her nightgown off her shoulders onto the floor, revealing the high, firm breasts and flat stomach she had before the children came.

"You will always be young and beautiful to me, my bride," he said, sweeping her up in his arms and carrying her back to bed.

* * * *

"Where's my husband?" Dolly asked for the third time.

What irked Ruth wasn't the repetition; it was the word "husband." Dolly had always called him Sol or Daddy. Husband sounded so formal, as if Ruth were a stranger. Maybe that's what I am to her now.

"Mom," Ruth said, reinforcing her familial position, "Daddy's not here."

That's as far as she would go. Reminding Dolly that Sol was in the ground would've been cruel.

"But he was here last night."

Here we go again, Ruth thought. Dolly smiled in merriment. Her eyes twinkled. And just as suddenly, they were vacant.

"Mom?"

"What, Sweetheart?"

"You were saying…?"

Dolly stared at her fingernails.

"I don't remember."

82

22

"Should we call the police?"

"And say what?" said Naomi's husband. "That our twenty-year-old daughter wants to have a *life?*"

"I haven't heard from Shoshanna in over a week. She doesn't answer my calls. Anything could've happened. We never should've gotten her that apartment."

"No, we should've locked her in her bedroom when she started to menstruate and not let her out until we arranged her marriage."

Lately, sarcasm was Howie's automatic default. Naomi suspected it had something to do with resentment over her book sales. He slid his moo shoo over to Naomi's side of the kitchen table. They ate kosher vegetarian Chinese every night of the week except on Shabbat when Naomi made *cholent*, slow-cooked cement that gave Howie gas for a week.

"If you had just given her some *space*, she never would've left," he said.

Howie and his "space." He used it to rationalize his nightly ramblings and phone calls behind closed doors. She wasn't going to fight that battle now. She threw on her purple poncho and grabbed her keys.

"Where are you going?" Howie asked.

"To find *our* daughter."

Howie waited until he heard the elevator open and close, then flipped open his cell phone.

"All clear. The Mother Ship is in orbit." he said.

* * *

Naomi pushed the intercom for Apt. 3-B.

"Who is it?" said a shrill female.

"Mrs. Karp, Shoshanna's mother."

There was a long, agonizing pause, followed by a buzz, letting her into the building on West 26ᵗʰ Street. It was just a formality. Naomi had a duplicate key. She climbed the three floors, stopping to catch her breath at each landing. No elevator. But at least it was a clean building with freshly painted halls and no weird smells. Naomi was prepared for Shoshanna's indignation, her anger and contempt, the usual punishment.

"Hi, Mrs. Karp? I'm Karla? And this is Zara and Suki?"

Naomi had never seen these girls or heard their names before. Their hair colors came from a Crayola box. Pink. Orange. Green.

"Is Shoshanna here?" Naomi asked.

"No," said Orange Hair.

"Well, who are you and what are you doing here?"

The Crayola Heads conferred amongst themselves, then Pink Hair volunteered, "Uh, well. We're her roommates?"

It was a one-bedroom apartment. Where did they all sleep? And why hadn't Shoshanna told her that she was splitting the cost of the apartment for which Naomi paid.

"How do you know my daughter?" she asked.

"She posted a flyer on the bulletin board at F.I.T.," said the one with a pink mullet.

If these are the fashion designers of tomorrow, God help us.

"Do you mind if I just wait here for her?" Naomi said, sitting down on a tangerine foam rectangle. The girls eyed one another nervously.

"Well, she doesn't stay here anymore," said Pink Hair.

Naomi felt the room spin and a pin-ball hammer start to work on her frontal lobes.

"What do you mean she doesn't live here? Where is she?"

Pink Hair went into the kitchen and came back with an address scribbled on a piece of yellow lined paper.

"This is where we send the rent?" she said.

Trembling, Naomi looked at the address. It was on the Upper East Side.

"May I use your bathroom?" Naomi asked.

She stared at her reflection in the mirror and said, "I deeply and completely accept myself." She flushed the toilet and slid open the medicine cabinet, grabbed a lipstick, a nail polish and birth control pills, tucking them into the voluminous folds of her cape. Naomi's kleptomania wasn't about taking things she needed. It was about restoring balance in the universe.

23

"You never talk about Nando," Miri said. "Are you separated or what?"

They were in the den watching television and Ellen DeGeneres had just limboed over her coffee table. Ruth could've bobbed and weaved her way out of the subject but rain had been whipping the windows for days and she was in the mood to vent.

"I was in the kitchen preparing dinner. Trader Joe's Chipotle Tilapia," said Ruth. "Nando went into the bedroom to call his mother in Brazil. He called her often. I thought he was a loving son. When dinner was ready, I called him. He didn't answer. So I went to the bedroom and found him in bed, on the phone, with his pants around his ankles and his thing in hand. He was…you know."

"Jeez," said Miri. "What did he say?"

"He said he was having phone sex."

"With his *mother*?"

"He claimed it was a sex hotline advertised in *LA Weekly.* Said he had never done it before."

"Right," Miri snorted.

Ruth fast forwarded over details that would cast her in a less than complimentary light. Hurling sizzling fish filets at her husband's exposed genitalia. Nando screaming, running cold water on his tender parts. Ruth screaming.

"I guess we had gotten kind of loud. Our neighbors called 911 and reported domestic violence. A cop showed up. Before I got a word in, Nando said I had tried to kill him." Ruth skipped over the fact that, at the time, Nando was holding a bag of frozen spinach to his inflamed crotch.

"The cop was Latino," she continued. "He and Nando started speaking Spanish. Next thing I knew, they stepped outside. Two Latinos commiserating over a ball-busting woman, right? Ten minutes later, Nando came back inside and apologized to me. He swore he'd would never do it again."

Miri nodded empathetically. She had been married for over twenty-five years and knew that "never again" was a constantly moving target.

"The next day, I checked our phone bill. The number Nando had called wasn't a sex hotline. It was the same number he had been calling in Brazil almost every night since we got married."

"So it *was* his mother?" Miri gasped.

"Worse," said Ruth. "I called the number in Sao Paulo. A woman answered. I said, this is Nando Veloso's wife, Ruth, to whom am I speaking? She said, I'm Nando Veloso's wife, Cecelia."

"No!" Miri said, slapping her own cheeks.

"Nando had been married to Cecelia for ten years. To me, for three. She was his real wife. I was just his green card."

"Poor baby," cried Miri, throwing her arms around Ruth. "I hope you cut him up into little pieces and fed him to the sharks."

"My lawyer did, but not until after Nando had taken a victory lap on Rodeo Drive and destroyed my credit."

"So are you divorced or what?"

"Or what," groaned Ruth. "I couldn't get a divorce. According to the State of California, our marriage was invalid." Ruth honked into a Kleenex. "Please don't tell Mom. Not that she would remember five minutes later but I'd rather keep this just between us."

"Of course," Miri said. "Thank god you didn't have kids."

Easy for you to say, Ruth thought. Miri had three grown sons, a doctor, a lawyer and an Olympic skateboard champion who maintained residences in Jackson Hole, New York and Seattle. Ruth loved her cousins but had always assumed she would have children of her own. The fact that Naomi had succeeded where Ruth had failed was more than unfair. It was catastrophic.

"But I tried," she sobbed. "I tried and nothing happened. And now it never will."

"You don't know that," counseled Miri. "It could've been his fault. Maybe he had a snip job and didn't tell you?"

Ruth blubbered into a throw cushion. Miri couldn't make out what she was saying. It wasn't until Ruth ran off to the bathroom, threw up and came back with red eyes and a ravaged mouth that Miri got the whole story. During her last year with Nando, Ruth hadn't used any birth control. They had sex every night. Sometimes every morning. Whatever he lacked in scruples, Nando more than compensated for in enthusiasm. Ruth, however, didn't get pregnant. Cecilia did.

"From phone sex?" asked Miri.

"Nando visited his family in Brazil at Christmas. I thought 'family' meant his mother, brothers, sisters, cousins. It meant his wife and children. He already had a seven-year-old son and a daughter with Cecilia. Last Christmas, he knocked her up again."

"Son of a bitch," muttered Miri. "I'm not going to tell you that adversity makes you stronger because that's a bunch of crap. But I'm glad you're here, Ruth. Your mother needs you. So do I..."

Ruth looked expectantly at her aunt, waiting for the rest of the story. Was Miri having her own marital problems? Health issues? Financial troubles? Whatever she was about to reveal was cut off by a loud THUD. They raced into Dolly's room and found her dragging a large suitcase.

"Mom? What are you doing?" Ruth said.

"Packing," Dolly said.

"Why?" Miri said.

"I've had a nice time," said Dolly, "But I want to go home now."

Ruth and Miri exchanged a glance.

"Mom, this is home," said Ruth.

Dolly looked around doubtfully and shook her head.

"No, no, this isn't my home."

"Where is your home?" Ruth ventured.

"5201 Flatbush Avenue."

It was where Dolly had lived as a child.

24

Naomi charged into a glittering Park Avenue condominium, only to be stopped by a massive Nigerian doorman.

"Service entrance 'round back," he said.

"I'm Naomi Karp," she announced, "Shoshanna Karp's mother."

His heavy-lidded eyes gave away nothing.

"Ma'am, the lobby is for residents only."

"My daughter *lives* here," she said, holding out the now crumpled piece of paper.

There was a slight shift in his demeanor, a softening of the hard line of his mouth.

"She's expecting you?" he asked.

"No, but…but this is an *emergency*."

"Okay, ma'm. Okay," he said, going behind the desk to the phone. "You say name is Karp?" He looked up and down a list. "Nobody here with that name. Maybe you have wrong building?"

"But I have the apartment number, 16F."

"You must have a name. The resident must give permission."

This was too much for Naomi. She shook from the inside out, sobbing uncontrollably. I got a nut job on my hands, the doorman thought and, not wanting to deal with a heart attack and EMTs, he offered her a chair.

"Maybe the apartment isn't in her name? Maybe she's staying with a friend?" Naomi said, half talking to herself.

"You know the friend's name?"

Naomi shook her head and fished in her woven Guatemalan bag for Shoshanna's high school graduation picture. It showed a pretty Asian teen with plump lips, doe eyes and big hair.

"I know this girl," he said. Then something shut down in his face. "She doesn't live here. You have to go now. Lobby is for residents only."

Naomi started to stand, then felt dizzy and sat back down again.

"May I have some water?"

The doorman rolled his eyes. In another hour the big tippers would start arriving home. The last thing they wanted to see was a crazy old woman in the lobby.

"You sit. I get water. Then you go,"

Naomi nodded. As soon as the doorman went in search of water, she made a dash for the elevator.

* * * *

"What the fuck are you doing here?" Shoshanna said, opening the door but keeping the chain on.

"Baby! Oh, thank God! Baby! You're alive!" Naomi cried.

"Of course, I'm alive. Are you fucking nuts?"

"Oh, Sweetheart. You don't know. You don't know what I've been through. When I went to your apartment and they told me you were gone…"

"You had no right to go there." Shoshanna's voice went up a notch.

Naomi pulled herself together.

"No right? I *pay* for that apartment."

"And what exactly does that entitle you to? My fucking *life?*" Shoshanna yelled and slammed the door shut.

Naomi sank to the floor, her arms wrapped around her knees, rocking back and forth, repeating her mantra. That was how the doorman found her when he responded to Shoshanna's complaint of a vagrant in the hall.

25

Ruth reached blindly for her phone, scavenging the sheets, pillows, night table, rug, before finally finding it under her bed.

"H'lo?"

"What are you doing now?" croaked a stranger.

"Sorry," Ruth said. "You have the wrong number…"

"This isn't my writer Ruth Sheraton?"

Ruth sat up and looked at the clock. It was 2 a.m.

"Gabby?"

Gabby Lee summoned Ruth to her Upper East Side condo which had recently bumped up its prestige by rejecting an application from Lady Gaga.

"The board would love to get rid of me too," said Gabby, "I'm going to outlive those fuckers."

Debbie Sandler had presented herself as the gatekeeper of the show. Gabby didn't meet with the writers, she had said. But here Ruth was, summoned in the middle of the night to what appeared to be the court of Versailles. A massive crystal chandelier dangled from a dramatically high ceiling where winged cherubs frolicked. Dove grey walls shimmered with gilt molding and smoked mirrors. Pale yellow damask curtains hushed the sounds of traffic. The Louis XVI furniture wasn't repro. It was hand-picked by an interior decorator who specialized in transferring heirloom pieces from medieval French castles to Manhattan condominiums.

"I know it's a bit much but it's *me*," Gabby said.

In person, at two-fifty-five a.m., Gabby looked exactly as she did on television. Every apricot glossy curl in place. Flawless complexion. Upon closer inspection, Ruth realized Gabby was wearing a thick layer of stage makeup, including false eyelashes that curled almost to her brows.

"They're mink," she said. "I'm on PETA's Most Wanted list."

Instead of her signature white angora sweater, Gabby wore a flowing black chiffon peignoir, trimmed in marabou.

"When I was growing up, movie stars wore these. Now they dress like hookers, so I have them made to order," Gabby sighed. "Style has gone out of style."

Ruth was suddenly conscious of her own attire. Baggy sweater over faded jeans.

Two yappy Pomeranians, the exact same shade of apricot as their owner's hair, encircled Ruth's feet.

"Don't mind Ike and Tina. They don't bite. Much" Gabby said.

Gabby insisted on giving Ruth a tour of her condo, pointing out every design detail as if Ruth were writing an article for *Architectural Digest*. As they trooped through exquisitely appointed bedrooms, bathrooms, sitting rooms and parlors the size of skating rinks, Ruth got the feeling that Gabby was making a point. I am a star, I live LARGE. You are small. Don't forget it.

"It's lovely," Ruth said as they traced their way back to the living room. "But why did you want to see me at this hour? I could've come over during the day."

94

"No, dear. You couldn't." Gabby said, sinking into a puffy silk sofa. "I sleep during the day. Work at night. Showbiz hours, you know."

"But you do a morning program."

"Morning to you. End of the night for me." Gabby gave Ruth a searching look. "Don't tell me you were sleeping when I called?"

Ruth didn't tell her. A swarthy man with slicked back hair in a crisp white cotton jacket and black slacks silently swept into the room and placed a tray of canapés on the coffee table. Ruth hadn't seen him on the tour. Where did he come from?

"Munchies!" Gabby trilled. "Thank you Eduardo."

The canapés looked as if they had been snatched from a wedding reception at the St. Regis. Miniature blinis stuffed with Beluga caviar, tiny pyramids of foie gras on toast points, ceviche in shot glasses, crab cake sliders. Gabby made Ike and Tina "kiss Mommy" then rewarded them with foie gras. No wonder they were shaped liked beach balls. Eduardo reappeared with a bottle of Moet, popped the cork, filled two flutes and returned the bottle to a sterling ice bucket. If the goal was to impress Ruth, Gabby had succeeded. But Ruth was getting the feeling that what Gabby really wanted was an audience.

"Is it true you don't like to leave your apartment?" Ruth asked.

"There's nothing out there that interests me anymore," Gabby said, ignoring the dog lapping from her glass. "Sardis. Twenty-One. Lindy's. Elaine's. I used to walk into a room and fucking *own* it. All these new restaurants and bottle clubs with their bullshit waiting lists? How many are going to be here in ten years? Huh?"

"Well..."

"*None*. That's how many," Gabby said. "And all these no-talent reality show celebrities, where they gonna be five minutes from now?"

Holding her nose and pulling an imaginary toilet chain, Gabby gave a juicy Bronx cheer.

"Debbie says you think I'm crude and mean-spirited." Gabby said.

Ruth choked on her crab cake.

"You okay?" Gabby said, "Eduardo knows CPR."

Ruth nodded and turned crimson.

"The thing is, I *am* crude and mean-spirited," Gabby said. "Not as a person, mind you. As a performer. That's my *schtick*. At my age, being funny isn't enough."

Gabby Lee had been a TV personality when Ruth was a child but her face had been surgically frozen at forty.

"You want me to change my tone?" Ruth said.

"Fuck no!" Gabby said. "You're brilliant. One of the best writers I ever had. I just want you to understand. I like to spice things up a bit."

That's it? She could've told me that on the phone or via email. Ruth helped herself to a blini topped with sour cream and caviar.

"So, Ruth, tell me about yourself," Gabby said.

"Well, I've worked in television for seventeen years, mostly on the west coast and ...."

Gabby waved her hands as if shooing away gnats.

"No. No. No. I don't want your fucking resume. I want to know about *you*. Tell me about Ruth Sheraton."

Oh, crap. What could she possibly tell Gabby Lee? Certainly not about her failed marriage or her mother's memory loss. *Be entertaining, Ruth.*

"I'm currently seeing a man who made his fortune in the art world."

"Ah. The guy escorting you around town, taking you to all those shows." Gabby said, eyes wide with interest. "Is he a hottie?"

"In a Cary Grant sort of way. Silver hair. Very knowledgeable about culture."

"Gay, huh?"

"Oh, I don't think..."

"You fucked him?"

"Uh, no."

"He's gay," Gabby announced. "Trust me. My first husband Mel was gay. I was in denial for maybe ten seconds. I caught him making out with the best man at our wedding."

"How awful..." Ruth vaguely remembered reading something about Gabby's first husband accidentally hanging himself in an act of auto-eroticism. Or maybe he had had enough of Gabby's *schtick.*

"Only for the best man. Mel and I had a *terrific* marriage. Twenty-six years. He quit his PR job to become my manager." Gabby handed Ruth a photo in a silver frame.

"That's Mel and me on our twentieth anniversary."

"You were a handsome couple."

"Mel was an Adonis. Me? I was a plain girl with a filthy mouth. But he *got* me, you know?" Gabby's eyes watered. "Gay men make the *best* husbands. They just die too soon."

Gabby's words were starting to slur. It was going on four a.m. Ruth wanted to go home. Her eyes started to cross. It happened when she was very tired or drunk. It had taken all her energy to focus on one Gabby; now there were two. Both performing the same endless monologue. *If I could just close my eyes for a sec.* Ruth blinked, trying to get her eyes to uncross, but she felt so woozy. When she opened her eyes, she was lying on the beach in Santa Monica, gulls cried, children squealed, splashing at the ocean's tasseled edge. Her chin dropped onto her chest.

"Am I keeping you up?" Gabby said.

"NO. NO. I'm fine." Ruth opened her eyes as wide as possible.

"Go on, get the fuck outta here."

Ruth was horrified. How long had she been asleep? Had she snored? And yet, no matter what she had done, Gabby's rude dismissal seemed like overkill. *She's been yaking at me all fuckin' night. Why not invite me to sleep on the sofa? Why throw me out at this ungodly hour?*

Ruth stumbled out into the predawn. The only signs of life were empty ghost buses cruising up Madison and hunched figures in the shadows, rushing along from one bad idea to another. Icy fingers of winter encircled her neck and reached up the sleeves of her leather jacket. Ruth's bones had grown accustomed to the arid warmth of LA. No amount of clothing could stop her from shivering. She stared into the black and blue night, searching for the half-moon of an available taxi. Home. I want to go home, she thought. But was no longer sure where that was.

26

Shoshanna's fashion design career ended her first day of class at F.I.T. when she discovered that sewing was a required course. I don't want to be a fucking seamstress, she told the registrar. What Shoshanna wanted to be was rich. She knew this was not something that happens to people who sit at sewing machines. She got her tuition back in full; it wasn't the college's policy but they would do anything to get the screaming girl out of their office. Then, she tacked a notice on the bulletin board: Roommates Wanted. By squeezing four students into her one-bedroom apartment, she generated a sweet income of three grand a month, just enough to cover her clubbing and cocaine habit. Of course, a girl didn't have to pay cash for drugs. They were on the house as long as she didn't mind giving blow jobs in bathroom stalls. Big deal. It wasn't like she was making a sex tape and posting it on YouTube.

It didn't occur to Shoshanna to inform her parents, who had signed the lease and paid for the apartment and tuition, of her change in plans. They wouldn't approve. They never did. They were bottom feeders, worker bees, who didn't appreciate Shoshanna's innate entrepreneurial drive. More importantly, they were not her *real* parents. She owed them nothing.

With the hefty deposit she collected from her tenants, Shoshanna had professional headshots taken and posted them on Craigslist. "College student seeks generous benefactor.

Must have luxury apartment on Upper East Side." Girls she knew from the club scene had done this. How else could they afford their Jimmy Choos? Shoshanna wasn't afraid of the psychos. It was the white collar guys looking for a quickie she had to watch. To weed out the losers, she viewed the men who responded to her ad on a web cam before agreeing to meet at an uptown money pit like the bar at the Hudson Hotel. That's where she met Mohammed Nasiri, a Pakistani businessman who maintained lavishly furnished apartments in Manhattan and London.

Mo was charmed by her youth, exotic beauty and forthright manner. She wanted a nice place to live and a clothing allowance, a modest request for a man who regularly draped his wife and mistresses in 24 carat gold. Shoshanna was willing to overlook Mo's age, disturbingly close to her father's, his toupee and pot belly. After all, this wasn't a romantic hookup. This was business. What clinched the deal for Shoshanna was Mo's palatial condo in one of Manhattan's newest glitter domes, fifty-one stories of glass with river and park views. All the furnishings, walls and window treatments were white, "the color of purity" he explained, except for the master bedroom which was painted in gold leaf.

"I am here only one or two weeks a month. You're welcome to stay while I'm away," he said.

Shoshanna wrapped her arms around Mo's plump neck and kissed him full on the mouth, trying not to giggle.

"May I see?" he asked, making sweeping motions with both hands.

"You want me to take off my clothes?"

"Very much," he said, seating himself on the Roche Bubois sofa.

It was awkward without music. Shoshanna hummed *Bad Romance* and pulled her cashmere sweater over her head, careful not to get lipstick on it. She unzipped her bunny fur mini skirt and stood there in Ugg boots and Calvin Klein bra and thong.

"Continue, please," Mo instructed.

This is wrong, Shoshanna thought. I'm giving a free show.

"I don't feel comfortable with this," she said, grabbing up her clothes.

Mo, who had negotiated arms deals with the Taliban, the Somalis and Hamas, smiled and nodded amicably.

"Of course," he said, opening up his Guggi wallet. "I understand. Let's see if I can make this situation more attractive."

Shoshanna was speechless.

"This is for cab fare," he said, placing a one hundred dollar bill on the glass coffee table. "This is to cover the cost of dry cleaning your clothes," laying out another Benjamin Franklin. "And this is for being the most beautiful woman I have ever seen."

Shoshanna stripped down to her bare skin, not knowing where to put her hands. Mo's face clouded over.

"What is that?" he asked pointing to her breast.

Shoshanna looked down, half expecting to see a new mole. Gross!

"That thing around your neck," he said.

It was a tiny gold Star of David her grandmother had given her for her bat mitzvah.

"You're not....?" he asked.

"Hey, man. This is New York. *Everyone's* Jewish," she deadpanned.

Mo slapped his thigh and howled. This was the funniest joke he had ever heard. A Chinese Jew! Tears poured out of his eyes. Shoshanna laughed along with him, letting him form his own conclusions.

The very next day, she moved into Mo's condo. He spent most of his time at his office, leaving her free to use his credit card to fill up her walk-in closet and get waxed and polished at uptown spas. The sex wasn't as yucky as Shoshanna anticipated. Mo knew how to please a woman.

Mo had a lot of rules. She wasn't allowed to touch his laptop, answer the door or invite friends over. Shoshanna didn't mind. He wasn't around to enforce them most of the time. Which is why, after a few weeks, she invited her two best friends for a sleepover. Mo was in London. Naturally, Shoshanna's BFFs invited their BFFs, so by midnight, hundreds of kids were hanging from the chandeliers, snorting coke and hurling water-filled condoms from the balcony.

Around midnight, a hunkie guy in a police uniform arrived and flashed a badge.

"Oh, are you going to put handcuffs on me because I've been baaaad?" Shoshanna asked, assuming he was a stripper.

"Ma'am? We received a call from the owner of the apartment, Mr. Nasiri."

Shoshanna stopped smiling.

"He's not here. He's out of the country," she said.

"I know, ma'm. He's watching his property on surveillance cameras and he doesn't like what he sees.

You're going to have to ask your guests to leave the premises immediately."

* * *

Shoshanna slept for the better part of the next day and when she finally surveyed the damage, she knew her arrangement with Mo was over. Merry Maids would clean up the booze, pizza stains and vomit. It would take more than Lysol to remove the graffiti from the gold leaf walls. Shoshanna called the coffee shop on the corner and asked them to deliver a double espresso and an extra large OJ. She was so dehydrated, she would've taken her coffee intravenously. When the doorbell rang, Shoshanna threw on a bathrobe, thinking it was the delivery guy. It was her mother. FUCK. *Cannot deal with Psycho Mom now.*

Shoshanna rang her fingers over the glass topped dining room table in search of a white powder that was not an artificial sweetner, then popped open her I-pad and read the classifieds in the *Voice* for her next gig. Not another live-in position. Too confining. Too many "rules."

Female models wanted to work in hospitality industry. Excellent pay for right individual. Must be open-minded. That sounded right. When she showed up at the Tip Top Employment Agency for her interview, a woman with maroon hair took her photo and gave her forms to sign.

"They're looking for Asian girls but they can't say that in the ad because it's discriminatory," said the woman.

Shoshanna assumed the job involved sex. They said open-minded, right? Probably a massage parlor or escort service, she thought.

"Have you worked in the food service industry before?" the woman asked.

Food service? The thought of waitressing made her gag.

"How much does this pay?" Shoshanna asked.

"Five hundred an hour, plus tips."

27

"Hi. Is Grandma here?"

Ruth was tempted to say, "No, she's skiing in Gstaad." This was the first time Shoshanna had stopped by since the funeral.

"She's in the den," Ruth told her niece.

"I have something personal to discuss with Grandma," Shoshanna said.

Ruth got the hint. Shoshanna was here to make a cash withdrawal. God knows, Naomi couldn't afford that shearling coat her daughter was wearing.

"Fine. I'll be in my room," she said.

"Why don't you take a break and go out for a while? It's a beautiful day." Shoshanna said. "I'll keep her company for an hour or two."

Not one to dismiss a random act of kindness, Ruth grabbed her coat and headed for the park. The laughter of children provided a much needed counterpoint to the situation. Ruth had been coming to the same bench with her book and a large mocha latte often enough to know which kid was the sandbox bully and which one cried inconsolably if another child touched his truck. She also knew which nanny was writing an exposé about her employer, which mom had a yeast infection and which dad was into the kind of swinging not associated with playgrounds.

"Which one is yours?" asked a whippet-thin woman with boyishly short hair.

"None of them," Ruth said.

The woman's eyes narrowed with suspicion. Ruth quickly added, "I take care of my mother. She lives across the street."

The woman nodded, relieved that Ruth wasn't a predator.

"I'm Margot. That's my daughter Bethany."

She pointed at a little girl pouring imaginary tea for her teddy bear.

"She's adorable," Ruth said.

Little Bethany had a sprinkling of freckles across her pert nose and strawberry blond bunny tails and she was managing her tea party with the aplomb of an experienced hostess. Ruth had not meant her comment to elicit the story of Margot's life; she wanted to read two more chapters of the Connelly mystery before going back to the apartment. But Margot was in a sharing mode. In broad strokes, she described her career as an art director of a cutting edge ad agency, a buyout by a multi-national corporation, a childless starter marriage, an affair with a married man who dumped her for a younger woman, and her decision, on her forty-second birthday, to be a single mother.

"Best thing I ever did," snapped Margot, gazing at her daughter who was solemnly burying her teddy bear in the sandbox.

Ruth was impressed. Hollywood was rife with single women who adopted babies that had been carried to term by surrogates or purchased from Third World countries where a cow had more value than one more female infant. Invariably, these women were famous actors for whom pregnancy was an inconvenience, messing up their shooting schedules and figures. They paraded their African and Haitian children in front of the *paraparazzi*, then quickly dispatched them into the waiting hands of undocumented nannies. Margot, on the other hand, was a self-made woman who had done it all on her own.

"How did you…?" Ruth started to ask.

"In vitro," Margot said. She gave Ruth an appraising look. "Do you have children?"

It was Ruth's least favorite question, but park benches are neutral territory, the Swiss banks of regret.

"When I was young and not ready to start a family, I got pregnant and had an abortion. When I was finally ready, it just didn't happen."

Margot put a consolatory hand on Ruth's arm.

"It's not too late," Margot said.

Oh, but it is, Ruth thought. Her pregnancy had been a casting couch fiasco. A fading star of television westerns had invited her to meet "important people" at his Hollywood Hills ranchero. When she arrived, no one was there beside Bronco Billy and his best friend Jack Daniels along with cocaine, marijuana, a kidney-shaped pool and a full moon. Billy stripped naked and dove into the water. He suggested she do the same. At the time, it seemed like a great idea. Ruth had only been in town for a week and here she was under the stars. Literally. The abortion was a no-brainer. She was twenty-six with her entire life ahead. She would have a child when the time and man were right.

The right time came and went with all the wrong men, including the one she married. When Nando confessed that the "sister," with whom he conducted marathon phone conversations in Portuguese every night, was sort of, kind of, in a manner of speaking, his WIFE, Ruth looked for the diamond in the pile of shit. She wanted a child more than she wanted Nando. He not only had a wife in Sao Paulo, but three children and another on the way. Meaning, he had the *goods*. They struck a deal. He agreed to get her pregnant before going back to his *esposa* as long as he wouldn't be financially obligated for the child's support.

She imagined the new life growing inside her with Nando's curly dark hair, caramel skin and dimples. Four weeks later, Ruth got her period and crawled into bed. She didn't come out for two days. It's not him, it's me, she thought, I'll *never* have a child.

When Margot rushed off to referee a shoving match, Ruth made her getaway, vowing not to return.

28

To Ruth's amazement, Shoshanna's devotion to Dolly was consistent. She came to the apartment once or twice a week to "play beauty shop" with Grandma, giving Ruth an opportunity to go to the library or bookstore. Some women cannot be without a man. Ruth Sheraton could not be without a book. Which is why, on an unseasonably pleasant February evening, Ruth asked Larry to watch Dolly "for just a few minutes" while she ran out to buy the newest Michael Connelly. His detective novels were set in LA and she enjoyed eavesdropping on cops and crooks in the bars and hangouts she knew so well. Musso and Franks, Pinks, The Dresden.

"I'll be back in no time," she said.

And she would've if she hadn't found something she wasn't looking for in Contemporary Fiction. Alejandro Rey.

"I was hoping you'd come," he said.

Alex flapped his arms, a movement Ruth recognized from the playground. Kids did this when they were happy or excited. They flapped. Why was Alex flapping? In a silky white shirt, black vest and faded jeans with a burgundy muffler draped around his neck he did not look like a guy who put out the trash.

"The reading doesn't start for a few minutes," he said. "Have coffee with me."

His *reading?* Holy shit. Ruth had been impressed by his writing but had no intention of being a groupie.

"Sure," she said. "But I can't stay. I have to get back to my mother."

"How's she doing?" Alex asked.

Ruth couldn't think of a way to describe the staccato rhythm of her mother's days, moments of startling lucidity, encased in the fog of forgetfulness.

"Fine, thanks for asking."

Over cappuccino and biscotti, Ruth discussed his writing.

"You have a great sense of rhythm," she said. "The beat within the sentence. So many writers don't get that."

"Thank you," he nodded. "That's quite a compliment coming from you."

"Me?"

"Don't be modest. You've had a career I can only dream about."

Ruth wanted to say but you're still *young.* Thanks to Google, it was impossible to be coy about their age difference. She was almost ten years older than Alex and she suspected he knew it.

"Writing careers evolve," she said. "Give yourself time."

Alex stared wistfully into his espresso.

"Time is a luxury. I have a five year old son. My mother takes care of him but she's getting up there in years."

A son, a mother. Where was his wife?

"Do you have children?" he asked.

Christ. What is it with New Yorkers?

"Not yet," she said, because "no" elicited more sympathy than she wanted.

Alex flipped open his phone to check the time.

"I better go," he said.

Chairs were already filling, mostly by women, some young and dewy, others older, with reading glasses dangling on beaded chains around their necks. Almost all had Alex's book nesting in the warmth of their lap. As he moved toward the podium, the audience chatter quieted. They gazed upon Alex with shining eyes, their lips parted in expectation. A book store employee with a shaved head and corks in his ear lobes introduced Alex and reminded his captive audience of upcoming events featuring a celebrity chef, a celebrity designer and a woman who had attained celebrity status by having sex with celebrities.

"Good evening," Alex said softly, adjusting the microphone. He put on a pair of rimless glasses and opened his book. Ruth stood in the back. She had no need to see Alex, she just wanted to hear his voice.

"I don't remember learning how to mambo," he said. "My mother tells me I started dancing in my crib, holding onto the bars, bouncing in time to the music. This was not the case for the middle-aged couples from White Plains who signed up for private dance lessons at the resort where I worked the summer I turned twenty-one. For me, it was an opportunity to pay off my student loans. For the couples, it was something to do in between endless meals."

Ruth had recognized Alex's talent when she read his stories, but hearing him read aloud was a different matter altogether. Alex not only had the literary chops, he had an incredible voice, deep and resonant. He knew how to speak softly to make an audience lean toward him, how to tease out the humor and deadpan the punch line. They laughed on cue, sighed knowingly, clucked with recognition. He *had* them. Ruth could feel heat emanating from female fans as their estrogen level soared, dampening their foreheads with perspiration and lighting up their eyes with a wild gleam. *Get me out of here before they tear off his clothes.*

She eased her way out of the crowd and speed-walked to the El Coronado as if being chased by rabid dogs. Ruth was proud of herself. Men like Alex - artsy, sexy men with facile minds and agile bodies - had sidetracked her before and where did it lead? No, not this time. Not with Dolly as helpless as a child. Not with a mature, responsible, financially stable man like Dewitt Hogworth in her life. She quickened her pace, eager to climb into bed with Michael Connelly.

* * *

"Thank god you're here," Dolly cried.

Ruth looked from her mother to Larry and back again. What the hell had happened in the short time she was gone?

"Where have you been?" Larry said, hands on the hips of a vintage white bouclé Chanel suit. "I've been waiting almost an hour."

He was wearing a new wig, a blunt-cut caramel bob that called to mind Anna Wintour.

"Oh. Please. I wasn't gone that long," Ruth wanted to strangle her brother with his ropey pearls. Instead, she planted a kiss on top of her mother's head.

"If this keeps up, I'm going to have to make *other* arrangements for Mother," he said.

"Shut up, Larry."

"WHAT did you say?"

"You heard me. Shut the fuck up. I said I would be here at eight. So I'm a few minutes late. If there are any arrangements to be made, *I'll* make them."

"The hell you will!"

Larry stormed out, slamming the door behind him. Dolly trembled. She had always avoided conflicts. Now, with her dementia, loud voices terrified her. Ruth took her mother into her arms and rocked her like a baby.

"*Shah shah.* It's alright, Mom. It's alright," Ruth said.

Her words were instinctive, primal. The same calming mantra her mother had recited when she was a child. It had felt good to stand up to Larry. But underneath her bravado Ruth was afraid. Cancer, you can fight. Heart disease, you can fight. There are treatments, alternatives, second opinions. But Dolly was sinking into oblivion. Ruth was afraid that if she held on too tightly to her mother, she too would be pulled under. At the same time, she was aware that Dolly's increasing dependence on her provided something she had always wanted. Her mother's unconditional love. Perhaps Katya was right. Not that the Sheraton children had been neglected. But their mother's love had been spooned out carefully over the years, making sure that each child got their fair share, always leaving the biggest chunk for Sol. Now with Sol gone, along with Dolly's memory, Ruth was in a position to gorge on her mother's undivided attention. She led her by the hand to the den and sat next to her. Dolly was all smiles again, the shouting match with Larry forever lost in the bottomless well of forgetfulness.

"Mom, do you know how beautiful you are?" Ruth asked.

Dolly shrugged, her lips forming an impish grin. That was the source of her beauty, that she wore it so lightly, like a summer cardigan thrown carelessly over her shoulders. She had never been aware of it. No matter how many times her husband called her "gorgeous."

"How old am I?" Dolly asked. It was a question she asked with increasing regularity.

"You'll be eighty next month."

"Eighty?" Dolly gasped. "That's *old*."

"Well, I'm forty-two."

"NO! That can't be."

"Your hands look younger than mine," Ruth said. "Did you *ever* wash a dish?"

Dolly howled with laughter. This was one of the little games they played, knowing full well that Dolly had washed thousands, perhaps millions of dishes. Lately, it took so little to make Dolly laugh and even less to make her cry. They watched the over-sized, flat screen TV that Larry had bought in spite of Dolly's insistence that the old one worked fine. Dolly's eyes began to close. Ruth helped her mother change into a blue flannel nightgown and eased her into bed.

"You can sleep with me. There's room," Dolly said, indicating what had been Sol's side of their king-size bed.

"I'll keep you company just for a little while," Ruth said.

As she pulled back the sheets, the lavender and musk scent of her parent's marital bed brought back childhood memories of Sunday mornings when Ruth had had Mommy and Daddy all to herself.

"I feel safe when you're here," Dolly murmured, taking her daughter's hand.

Jesus. If Naomi could see this.

"I know, Mom."

"Whither thou goest, I shall go," said Dolly.

These were lines Dolly had memorized for a Biblical play at her neighborhood center as a teenager. It had such a profound effect on her that she named her daughters after the leading roles, Ruth and Naomi. Ruth had heard her mother speak these lines many times before and knew her cue.

"Whither thou liest, I shall lie," Ruth said.

"Thy people shall be my people," Dolly replied.

"Thy God, my God."

29

"It's just a pen," Witty said.

"Yes, but from Tiffany's."

Ruth wasn't used to receiving expensive gifts from men. Past lovers had made her compilations of Balkan music, surreptitious sex videos and one had wooed her with a leg of lamb. But no one, other than her mother and girlfriends, had ever spent money on her. Witty, however, rarely showed up without artisan chocolates, lavish bouquets or a thoughtful gift for Dolly. Ruth didn't know how to respond. She had been seeing her "young man," as Dolly referred to fifty-year-old Dewitt Hogworth, for several months. Lunch on Wednesdays at MoMA or the Harvard Club. Dinner and theatre, opera or the ballet on Saturday night, plus charity galas for which Ruth combed the racks of consignment shops for gowns that didn't make her look like the world's oldest bridesmaid.

Witty gravitated toward splashy venues and made a point of introducing Ruth to a dozen people before they reached their seats. If she had been reading the society columns, she would've known that she and Witty were an "item." But Ruth was so frazzled by her role as Dolly's protector that she hardly glanced at the headlines, let alone peruse gossip columns. If anyone had suggested that her relationship with Witty was becoming serious, Ruth would've howled. Their evenings ended with a chaste hug and a peck on the cheek. He called her "Dear," phoned at least once a day and held her hand in public. She assumed Witty was gay in that discreet Old Money way. What else could explain his passion for the arts, droll banter and disinterest in sex? He needed her for appearances. She was there for show, not tell. But the gifts, really, they had to stop.

"But, Darling, you're a writer," he said. "Do you think Hemingway used a Bic?

"Well, it is lovely. It's just that you do so much for me, I don't know how to reciprocate."

"Ah, Ruth, Ruth," he murmured. "You have no idea how much your friendship means to me."

Friendship. There it was. The invisible electric fence that demarcated the physical and emotional boundaries of their relationship. *God, am I at that age already? The age of tepid relationships of convenience?* She let out a long, languid sigh, then caught herself. *Get off the pity pot, Ruth. Would you rather be home watching Law and Order in your jammies, eating take-out from Happy Panda?*

Witty's car cruised through the snow-covered park on their way to dinner and turned south on Fifth Avenue. Ruth was surprised. They rarely dined below 60th Street.

"Where are we going?" she asked as they swept past the windows of Bergdorf's, Bendel's, then Saks.

"It's a surprise."

The car pulled over to the curb at Cajun Cabin, a barbecue joint in Chelsea. The ambience was cozy, in sharp contrast to the ostentatious restaurants Witty usually selected. There was no hand-shaking, head-nodding or eyeballing on the way to a corner table. No one jumped out of their seat to greet them. Ruth was charmed but confused.

"Have you been here before?" she asked.

"No."

"What made you decide to try it?"

"Katya said you would like it. Do you?"

"Very much," Ruth said, wondering if Katya was on commission. Her name came up with such regularity, it was starting to feel like a ménage a trios.

"Excellent. I want tonight to be *special.*"

Witty ordered oysters and a pulled pork sandwich. Ruth had blackened swordfish with pineapple salsa and garlic mashed potatoes. Instead of a pricey wine, they had icy mugs of draft beer. She had never seen Witty eat anything messy and watched with amusement as he chased strings of goo around his plate.

"If you don't get dirty, you're doing it wrong," he quipped, wiping his greasy hands on a napkin. "Is it all over my face?"

"Yep." Ruth dabbed her napkin in ice water and leaned across the table to remove gobs of sauce from Witty's cheeks.

"No fair," he said. "You have to get dirty too. Take a bite."

He held out the dripping pork sandwich. Ruth took a bite; sauce squirted all over the table.

"Happy now?" she asked with a full mouth, mopping up bits of gravy on her arms and face.

"Totally. Have you forgiven me for buying you something at Tiffany's?"

"All is forgiven," she said.

"Good," Witty said, "Otherwise you might not like dessert."

When espresso arrived, Witty placed a tiny blue box on the table. Ruth had had more beer than usual and was feeling too fuzzy to ponder the implications. Witty had given her a cashmere wrap for Christmas. But this was the middle of February. What's the occasion? Lincoln's birthday?

"Happy Valentine's Day," Witty said, pushing the box toward her.

OMIGOD! Valentine's Day! Witty had gone to all this trouble and she had nothing for him, not even a card.

"Oh, I'm so embarrassed. I've been so preoccupied."

He reached across the table and cupped her chin with his hand.

"Of course, you've been preoccupied. You're caring for your mother. Now open it."

Inside the little blue box was an even smaller black velvet box with cream satin lining.

"Do you like it?" he said. "Katya helped pick it out. If you want a different setting…."

If the waiters had clustered around the table and sang, Ruth wouldn't have noticed. This was no friendship ring. It was a brilliant, four-carat, pear-shaped, white diamond. She had never seen a perfect diamond but had a feeling this was the real deal.

"I don't know what to say," she gushed.

"You don't have to say anything. Just give me reason to hope."

Ruth put the ring on her finger. What else could she do with all the patrons and staff eagerly watching? Then, the most awful thing happened. Everyone *applauded* as if she had just accepted a proposal. She hadn't. Had she? A bottle of Moet, compliments of the house, appeared. Witty and

Ruth clicked glasses. More applause. *Oh, God, this is so embarrassing.* The ring was a perfect fit. *How did he know? Oh, right. Katya, my silent partner.* Ruth had never been engaged. During her sham of a wedding, she and Nando had exchanged mood rings from the Dollar Store. At the time, it was hilarious. Now, as she snuck sidelong glances at the diamond, Ruth was bedazzled. It seemed as if the Northern Lights were emanating from her left hand.

* * * *

Ruth meant to talk to Witty about the ring as soon as they got into the car. But he was so ebullient, she decided it could wait.

"How about a nightcap at my place?" he said.

No harm in that. Ruth had been to Witty's penthouse during the day to admire his art collection, a mix of limited edition prints, Ansel Adams photographs and mid-century American paintings, including a Rothko and a small but important Warhol. She had never been there at night and was unprepared for breath-taking aerial perspective with all of Manhattan glittering below.

"I feel like I'm flying," she said, her arms spread like wings.

"Here. This will help you maintain altitude." Witty handed her a glass of Frangelico on the rocks and lead her to the red leather sofa, the only stroke of color in the black and white room. An Offenbach concerto played softly. Witty placed his hand on her knee. The fireplace glowed and the lights of Manhattan twinkled north, south, east and west.

"I am a complicated man, Ruth, but I believe I can offer you the kind of life you deserve. You value your independence. I value mine. You're devoted to your mother and I admire that greatly. If you enter into the partnership of matrimony with me, I promise that your mother will have the best care…"

Witty's tone suggested an investment opportunity, not a marriage proposal. Yet, there was a drop dead diamond on her hand. It *did* look so lovely. It would've been heartless to give it back to him just now. She would find a way to let him down gently. Tomorrow.

And yet. Ruth wasn't blind to the advantages of such an arrangement. When Witty spoke of independence she knew exactly what that entailed; she would be free to engage in discreet affairs and so would he. Hollywood was rife with gay stars who entered into platonic marriages with women eager to share their mega-mansions and lucrative pre-nups. Ruth had read enough Jane Austen to know that pragmatism trumps romance when a woman of a certain age is of limited means.

"Witty, I don't want anyone to take care of my mother. I want to do it myself."

"Of course you do, Darling. Mother will live with us."

Ruth's mouth dropped open and Witty stuck his tongue in it. He tasted, quite pleasantly, of Frangelico. With one hand, he unzipped his pants and, with the other, he unhooked her bra.

* * * *

Ruth had not had sex in almost a year. Even an inexperienced, awkward lover would've pleased her, but when Witty scooped her up in his arms and carried her to his bed, Ruth found herself in the hands of a surprisingly artful lover who did not focus on his own needs until he had satisfied her. Repeatedly.

Not once, in all their prior evenings together, had Ruth wondered what was under Witty's tailor-made, Egyptian cotton shirts and Brioni slacks. Now she knew. Witty was ripped. Sinewy muscle, head to toe.

"Have you always been like this?" she asked, running her hand over his steely abs.

"God, no," he laughed. "I was the fat boy at Phillips. The last to be chosen for team sports. I didn't start to exercise until I was in my forties."

"What motivated you?"

Witty sat up in bed, carefully draping the Porthault sheets.

"Fear," he said.

"Of what? Heart disease?"

"No. You're probably wondering why I haven't taken my socks off," he said.

Actually, Ruth hadn't paid any attention to Witty's feet; it was his other appendages that had kept her occupied for the past three hours. He peeled off his socks. A boxy device was strapped around one ankle.

"I have to wear the damn thing for another six months," he said.

Between the sheets, men had sprung all sorts of surprises on Ruth. Penis pumps. Pearls that would never grace a neck. Handcuffs. Whatever gets you through the night was her motto. But she couldn't fathom the erotic potential of this black plastic gizmo. Did it vibrate? Emit electric shocks? Increase blood flow to his penis?

"What is that?" she said.

"A parole monitor. I made some bad business decisions which I deeply regret, for which I served six years."

"You were in *prison*?"

Ruth pulled the sheets up to cover her breasts and inched away from him. *I'm gonna kill Katya.*

"It was a minimum security correctional facility in upstate New York, practically a country club. Most of the inmates were professionals. Guys like me who had taken bad advice."

"You mean white collar crime?"

"White collar crime is the accountant who skims off the top. This was yacht club crime. High rollers, living large, who fell victim to their own egos."

"What exactly did you do?"

"Well, we had access to the Internet, there was a wonderful library and we organized a softball team."

"No," Ruth said, scrunching up her knees to put more distance between herself and Witty, "I meant what did you *do* that landed you in jail?"

"Oh. I don't want to bore you with the legalese."

"Go ahead. Bore me."

Ruth bit her lip, preparing for the worst. Pedophile. Blackmailer. Arsonist. Thief. What was it they always said on the six o'clock news? He *seemed* like such a great guy.

"When I came out of Harvard I wasn't really sure what I wanted to do. Wall Street and banking, where most of my friends worked, struck me as one big rodeo. The art world was sexier. I got an internship at Sotheby's and was mentored by Hassan Maloof, an expert in contemporary painting. He took me under his wing, introduced me to major collectors and to the best forgers in the world."

"Forgers? Why would someone at Sotheby's associate with forgers?" Ruth asked.

"Because that was Hassan's specialty, protecting Sotheby's clients from master forgeries. But he had a side business, providing oil sheiks and Russian industrialists with magnificent reproductions of works that hung in the Louvre and the Prado. It was legal. The buyers knew exactly what they were getting and were willing to pay hundreds of thousands, even millions for an undetectable copy of a masterpiece. But things got murky when he got in on the ground floor in Dubai. You can't imagine how much money was involved, Ruth. I grew up in Darien. We had *things* but nothing like the wealth that gushes out of the ground in the United Arab Emirates.

"The problem started when I left Sotheby's and became Hassan's partner, supplying reproductions to hotels in Dubai. I don't speak or read Arabic and somehow, things got out of hand. A hotel developer thought he had purchased the original *Nude Descending the Staircase*. When he found out he hadn't, I was arrested."

"You went to jail and Hassan went free?"

"It was complicated. But I carry no resentment. Hassan has been very generous. My penthouse was a gift. And my time away was a blessing in disguise."

Ruth noted that Witty never used the word *prison*.

"I had the opportunity to become friends with brilliant financiers, politicians and businessmen who, like me, had experienced a, uh, lapse in judgment," Witty said. "Splendid bunch of fellows. We get together once a month at the Harvard Club. But more importantly, I had time to reevaluate my marriage, which had ended rather abruptly following my arrest. I came out knowing what I really want out of life."

Ruth wanted to believe him. But her trust meter had been badly dented by Nando and, besides, no one gets sent to jail for "good behavior."

"If there's one thing I was guilty of," Witty said, allowing for a pregnant pause. "I was too *trusting*."

He kissed her forehead as if she were a child and within minutes he drifted into a deep, sonorous sleep. Ruth stared at the ceiling. First a bigamist, now a felon.

30

"You're overreacting," said Katya. "Give him credit for being honest."

"Honest? He didn't tell me until *after* we were in bed."

"So, he's insecure. He was afraid you'd reject him."

Katya addressed her comment to Ruth's diamond which was a half carat larger than her own. They were at Diva Nails waiting for their second coat of French Toast polish to dry. No more do-it-yourself manicures, she told Ruth.

"But he's a convicted felon. He went to prison."

"So what? The best people - Martha, Lindsay, Paris – they *go away* for a little while and come out with six-figure book and TV deals. It's practically a status symbol."

The manicurist kept her head down and said something in Korean to the girl next to her.

"They're talking about us," Ruth said.

"No, they're not. They don't understand a word we're saying. Why do you think you have to point to the colors? Just promise me you won't do anything stupid."

"Like what?"

"Like turn down the opportunity of a lifetime."

"But…:

Katya waved her glossy nails in the air.

"You're over forty and you have *nothing* to show for it," she said.

Before Ruth could answer, Katya plunged on.

"Dewitt Hogworth has paid his debt to society. It's not like he's a serial killer or a rapist. He *gets* you, Ruth. Think about it. Witty wanted to jump on your bones the moment you met. I was there. I saw it. But what did he do? He held back because you were in mourning. He pursued you for months, living on sheer hope."

"How do you know this?" Ruth asked.

"He's my friend. We talk."

"You talked to Witty about me?"

Katya rolled her eyes.

"Of course, I talked about you. The poor man was besotted."

Ruth thought back to all the times that Witty seemed to read her mind, choosing plays starring her favorite actors, buying the bittersweet chocolate-covered apricots she adored and knowing what color sweater she would like. Katya had been coaching him every step of the way. She probably went with him to Tiffany's to pick out the ring; he had said as much.

"What's wrong?" Katya asked.

"I thought I was in a relationship just between Witty and me. But it's been a threesome all along."

"What are you talking about? You went to bed with him. I didn't."

"Maybe you should."

Ruth struggled to pull the ring off her finger.

"DON'T!" Kayta yelped. "You'll ruin your nails."

Ruth removed the fabulous diamond from her hand and threw it into Katya's lap.

"I hope you'll be happy together."

* * * *

Ruth felt two-hundred and ten pounds lighter. No ring! No Witty! She knew where she had to go. What she had to do. Snow had melted into sludge, turning every curb in Manhattan into an Olympic broad jump. By the time she arrived at Alex's building, her jeans were splattered with icy muck.

"Sorry I couldn't stay for your reading the other night," she said. "My mother…"

"Sure. Sure. I understand," nodded Alex. His expression was in neutral gear, displaying neither enthusiasm nor annoyance.

"I'd like to talk to you about your writing," Ruth said.

His eyes lit up, then went blank.

"Okay. When?"

His tone was flat.

"Are you busy now?"

31

For fifteen minutes, Ruth spoke to Alex about his use of imagery and balance of dialogue and narrative. Then she stopped mid-sentence and kissed him full on the mouth. Waiting for a man to make the first made Ruth nervous. He tasted as she had imagined. Espresso, pepper and honey. She stood up and unbuttoned her blouse, tugged off her boots and jeans and pulled him down on top of her on the sofa.

"Does this mean your critique is over?" he said.

"No, it's just begun," she said, unzipping his jeans.

Alex did not put up a fight. He put an Astor Piazzolla tango on his M3 player.

* * * *

They laid breathless on his bed, bodies drenched in sweat as sweet as rain.

"What was that?" Alex asked.

"I don't know," she sighed.

But Ruth knew exactly what it was. Some people jump out of planes to experience exhilaration; Ruth was addicted to another kind of free fall, the excitement of jumping into the arms of the wrong man at the worst possible time. She had spent many fifty-minute hours exploring this. Her sexual encounter with Witty had occurred more out of gratitude – that diamond did not come out of a Cracker Jack box - than desire. It was vigorous but lacked the *frisson* Ruth required to feel alive. A smoldering Latino writer with a mysterious ex-wife was the empty pool into which she felt compelled to dive, head first, back arched, toes pointed.

Had Ruth really gone to Alex's to discuss the art of fiction? Well, yes. Of course, she had. If she had known – really known - that she was going to run her hand along his thigh while debating the pros and cons of the omniscient narrator, it wouldn't have been a spontaneous act of passion. And Ruth was nothing, if not spontaneous. If she had known they would rip off each other's clothes, she would've worn matching undies.

"I'd invite you to say overnight but my son...," Alex said.

"Oh, of course."

Ruth did the awkward dance of following the trail of her discarded clothes back to the living room. Alex pulled on jeans, sans underwear.

"Would you like to go out with me sometime?" he said, slipping his bare feet into moccasins.

"You mean a date?"

"I guess you could call it that." Alex stood close enough, she could smell herself on his breath. "Dinner. Dancing." His hands clasped her hips and drew her against him. They swayed without music.

"You move well," he said.

"I can follow a strong lead."

"If my son wasn't due home any minute, I'd dance you right back into bed."

Ruth agreed to dinner the following evening. If Alex had asked, she would've agreed to running down Columbus Avenue naked in freezing rain. As she left the building, a five-year old boy with curly black hair and huge brown eyes was coming up the stairs. An older woman in an orange wool coat stood on the sidewalk until the boy was safely inside, then quickly turned and walked toward Amsterdam Avenue. The woman did not return Ruth's smile.

32

Dolly shoved her hand between the mattress and box spring. They weren't there. Could they have fallen behind the bed? Or under it? With great difficulty, she pressed her head against the carpet and peered into the dark void. Nothing under the bed. Nothing behind it. Who could've taken them?

"I thought we'd go to Orchard Street today and get you a new bra. You're growing out of that one."

Dolly looked up. Bella, her mother, sat at the vanity table, applying a thick smear of maroon lipstick. Her squat, plump body was encased in a clinging pistachio knit dress, her swollen feet stuck into pink shoes. It was from garish sights such as this that Dolly developed a fondness for the calming effects of beige.

"What did you do with my letters?" Dolly cried.

"Letters? I don't know from any letters," Bella shrugged. "Put on some lipstick and comb your hair. We're going shopping."

This was her mother's answer to everything. Or rather, her way of avoiding everything. Shopping.

"I don't *want* to go shopping. I want my letters," Dolly insisted.

"I don't know what you're talking about," Bella sniffed, stuffing enough Kleenex in her purse to dry all the noses in Brooklyn.

"Yes you do. My letters from Frank. What did you do with them?"

"Frank? Frank who? Frank Sinatra?"

"MOTHER," Dolly wailed. "I'm not a child anymore. There's a war going on. Frank could be killed. These letters are all I have. Please…."

Bella stood up and wagged a finger in Dolly's tearful face.

"You listen to me and you listen good. As long as I'm alive, you are my child and no child of mine is going to ruin her life over an Eye-talian. If Frank dies in this lousy war, it'll be the best thing that ever happened to you. Someday you'll thank me. Now, fix your face and let's go."

Dolly ran into the bathroom and locked the door.

"I'm not coming out," she shouted. "I'm not going anywhere until you give me my letters. I'll starve myself."

"Go shit yourself," Bella, who was no fan of subtlety, hollered in Yiddish.

Dolly looked in the mirror. Her young face was shriveled, a landscape of crevices and craters. Her beautiful red hair was as white as snow with the blush of pink scalp peeking through. She clutched onto the sink to keep from falling to the floor.

"Are you locked in again, Miss Dolly?" a voice called from the other side of the door. "Shall I call the janitor?"

Dolly felt dizzy. She held onto the sink. That didn't sound like her mother's voice.

"Who is it?" Dolly called out.

"Miss Dolly, it's me, Geneva."

Geneva? That name sounded so familiar.

"Is my mother still there?" Dolly asked.

"No, Miss Dolly, there ain't no one here but me. Why don't you just unlock the door and we'll watch Hoda and Kathy?"

Dolly turned the latch and peered into the bedroom cautiously.

"You sure she's gone?" she asked.

"Yes, ma'am."

"She took my letters. Can you help me find them?"

"Yes, ma'am. But first let's go to the den and have some soup and crackers. How's that sound?"

"I'd like. I'd like that very much."

Geneva walked slowly with Dolly hanging on her arm, as if making her way up the center aisle of her church. Step. Pause. Step. Pause. Miss Dolly wouldn't use her cane or walker. She was too vain for that. Geneva understood. Old folks have their pride. The mind goes. But the pride holds tight until the good Lord calls you home.

33

Normally, Ruth used only lip gloss and mascara. Tonight she made use of her complete cosmetic arsenal and used an obscenely over-priced "glaze" on her hair that made it shine like an American Girl doll. She wore a navy silk slip dress that she picked up on sale at Zara with a pair of comfortable, low-heeled shoes. He had said *dancing.*

Alex had obviously gone to some trouble himself. He was closely shaven, dressed in a gray linen shirt, charcoal suit and he smelled like a rain forest. His choice of restaurant hit just the right note. Café Emilio was a small, below-street-level, Italian bistro on West 71st Street. They dined in the garden patio, a hidden oasis, lit by candles and warmed by heating lamps. Ruth was impressed. She had imagined he would take her to one of the nosey, ubiquitous eateries on Columbus where menus leaned toward the Trend du Jour, be it half-pound burgers on brioche or lobster roll.

"The best dishes aren't on the menu. May I order for both of us?" Alex asked.

When the waiter appeared, Alex shifted into Italian. Ruth had no idea what he was saying; the waiter grinned enthusiastically. A bread basket and a bottle of Motepulciano d'Abruzzo appeared.

"Where did you learn to speak Italian?" she asked.

"In bed." Alex let that hang in the air before adding, "My wife was from Milan."

"Where is she now?"

Ruth was feeling reckless. The wine helped.

"Milan. Her family is very, uh, influential. They never approved of our marriage and took every opportunity to lure her back to the nest. It took a few years, but they succeeded."

Alex downed his wine and refilled their glasses.

"She remarried?"

"To a man who owns all the knitting mills in Italy," Alex said in the rapturous singsong voice of someone telling a fairy tale.

"But your son lives with you?"

"In the winter. He spends summers with his mother."

Alex's son Paolo was five. His divorce was three years ago, just enough time to turn bile into sarcasm. To change the topic, she asked about his reading. Alex imitated one of his zealous fans, an intensely serious would-be writer, trying to extract literary secrets while obtaining the author's signature.

"They all think there is a metaphysical door through which they must pass in order to achieve literary success," Alex said. "I tell them, put your ass in the chair and words on the page. Everything else is bullshit."

I like this man. I really like him. Alex greeted the arrival of each course with a kiss to the circle made by the thumb and fingers of his right hand. First came crab ravioli in vodka sauce and *orecchiette* with sausage, then short ribs braised in Chianti with broccoli rabe. He tore off chunks of bread and mopped up his plate. Ruth did the same. Alex talked with his eyes and his hands, constantly touching her arm, her cheek, her knee, sending her endorphins on a carnival ride.

"I'm glad we had sex before our first date," Ruth blurted out.

"Me too," said Alex.

"I didn't mean that the way it sounded. I meant, I get nervous on first dates."

"Because you don't know what's going to happen, right?" he refilled her wine glass and his own. "I agree with you one hundred percent. This way we both can relax and enjoy the evening because we both know how it will end."

Alex stared into her eyes with a directness that wet her panties.

"Where did you get that hat?" he asked.

Hat? Ruth reached a tentative hand up to her head. *Oh, right.* It was a large black velvet rose in a poof of veiling that nested so lightly amid her curls, she had forgotten it was there.

"Oh, this?" she said. "I made it a long time ago."

It had been part of a Dorothy Parker costume for a Halloween party in college. Besides the hat, she had worn horn-rimmed glasses, ruby lipstick and carried a cocktail shaker in lieu of a purse. She had found the hat on the top shelf of her childhood bedroom closet, along with other remembrances of things past.

"So you're a writer and a hat designer? What don't you do?"

I don't cook, clean or have relationships that last longer than eighteen months. But why spoil a lovely evening?

* * * *

Ruth and Alex did not sleep together that night. His mother was babysitting at his apartment and Ruth wasn't about to sneak him into her bedroom at the El Coronado.

That's all Larry would need to declare her unfit to care for Dolly. But what transpired on the dance floor at Nasty, a new club in the meat packing district, was no less a mating ritual. The music – an eclectic blend of Latin, Middle Eastern and hip hop heavy on percussion - throbbed through the floor. Alex reeled her out and spun her back, starting out slowly to gauge her ability, then progressed gradually to more complicated, faster moves.

"You have Cuban rhythm," he said.

Nando had trained her well. Head high. Killer eye contact. Shoulders still. All the action remains below the belt. Knees loose. On the dance floor, they never lost contact with each other's gaze, hands or hips. And cruising uptown at 3 a.m. in the back seat of a Yellow Cab, Ruth's dress was around her waist, her fishnets all but ripped to shreds by Alex's teeth.

"I feel like I'm nineteen," she said, pulling herself together as they neared the El Coronado.

"Good," Alex said, "Growing old is bad for your health. You can die from it."

They kissed sloppily outside her building.

"Come to my place next Friday night," he said, "Paolo will stay at his cousin's."

He walked away backwards, waving, before breaking into a run towards Columbus Avenue. Ruth ducked past the concierge, relieved it was a new guy and not one of the regulars who had known her since childhood. Inside the elevator, she checked herself out in the mirror on the ceiling. *Jesus. I don't just feel nineteen. I look it.*

34

"My, my," Larry observed, "Don't we look well fucked."

Ruth smiled into her oatmeal. Nothing he said could bait her.

"Breakfast at noon?" chided Larry.

"Want some?" she asked, holding out a spoonful.

Larry hesitated, then put the spoon in his mouth.

"Hmmm, it's delish," he said.

"Brown sugar, vanilla, raisins and cinnamon. I use half and half instead of milk."

He joined her at the kitchen table just like when they were kids.

"You had a late night. Anyone special?" he asked.

"Just someone who makes me happy."

"Well, he has great taste in flowers," Larry said. "I put them on the piano."

Flowers? Alex sent flowers? Ruth flew to the living room. There they were, an all-white, aromatic bouquet of narcissus, roses and star gazer lilies. In February. How extravagant. The card read: *To the beginning of Forever.* Witty.

"It must've been some goodnight kiss" said Larry.

Ruth had awakened with a clear memory of everything that had happened the night before. Alex's hand grazing hers over dinner. The heat of his body on the dance floor. Those eyes. That mouth. What she had forgotten was that she was engaged to another man. The ring? She had to give it back to

Witty in a respectful, thoughtful manner. If he finds out that she wantonly threw it at Katya, he'll be crushed. Bad karma.

* * * *

"What did you do with the ring?" Ruth asked.

"I threw it in the East River." Katya dipped her pinkie into a tester of metallic eyeshadow at the Chanel counter at Bendel's and dabbed one eyelid.

"You didn't!"

"Would you like to try Rapelle for fine lines and wrinkles?" purred a salesgirl with a barely discernable Russian accent.

"Do I look as if I *need* it?" snapped Katya. Then to Ruth, "These idiots. Where do they get them?"

Katya marched briskly from the cosmetics department to accessories.

"No, really," pleaded Ruth. "What did you did with the ring? Did you give it back to Witty?"

Katya rifled through a display of Judith Leiber purses.

"I should have," she said. "You are the stupidest smart woman I know."

"I know. I know." Ruth said. "Do you have aspirin?"

Along with the return of her memory came a pounding headache and a terrible thirst. Katya dug into her limited edition Birkin and pulled out a vial of ibuprofen.

"Wow. 800 mg?" said Ruth.

"One of the perks of being married to a surgeon." Katya then unzipped a compartment inside her bag and held out her hand. In the palm was the pear-shaped diamond. As Ruth reached for it, Katya closed her hand into a fist.

"Do not embarrass me again, Ruth."

"I won't. I promise."

Katya slowly opened her hand. Ruth put the ring on her finger. For the remainder of the afternoon, salesgirls fawned over her, or more to the point, over her flawless diamond.

"You see," Katya said. "That's what Witty gives you. *Respectability.*"

Ruth smiled serenely and bought herself a sheer black lace bra and matching thong to wear on her next date. With Alex. She would give the ring back to Witty. Absolutely. Positively. But not just yet.

35

Magicians cut women in half all the time. To Ruth's surprise, it was a simple trick once she worked out the details. She saw Witty on Wednesdays and Saturdays, with the occasional Sunday brunch, and Alex on Tuesdays and Fridays. Sex with Witty was athletic but routine. In bed. Lights out. With Alex, every tryst was an episode of Wild Kingdom with a tango soundtrack. Just hearing the first moans of the accordion made her thighs tremble. While his mother and son went to the movies, Alex and Ruth devoured one another in the shower, on the kitchen floor, the dining room table, the sofa. Sometimes they didn't bother to disrobe. Other times, he tore her clothes off with such ferocity, she sauntered back to the El Coronado in his shirt and sweat pants.

She was careful to leave the diamond ring in her childhood jewelry box, a white leather case with red velvet lining in which a tiny plastic ballerina twirled to *Send in the Clowns*. The only moments of confusion were in the throes of orgasmic ecstasy. It is a discreet woman who cries out to God, rather than risk naming the wrong lover. This was not a problem when she was with Alex. But when Witty's ambitious thrusting exceeded her patience, Ruth mentally switched partners.

"Alex? No, no. I must've said Allah," Ruth explained. "I've been reading a lot of Rumi lately."

This is how men have managed things for centuries. They have wives whom they treat with respect and mistresses they fuck. Isn't that the way her own mother rationalized her father's womanizing? *I had my children. He had his whores.* Ruth sensed that she took after her father, perhaps in ways she had never fully understood. But her father had been in love with her mother, of this she was sure, and what he felt for other women had been no more than the thrill of the hunt.

Her attraction to Alex was more complicated. It was deeper, they *connected*. Often, when they lay on the floor in wonderment, waiting for their heartbeats to return to normal, they spoke of their innermost dreams and desires. He spoke of a screenplay he was writing about a Cuban American writer who fell in love with the daughter of a wealthy Italian industrialist. Ruth worried about the ending.

"Does the girl come back to the writer when he becomes rich and famous?" she asked.

"No. It's too late for that," he said, his hand drifting between Ruth's thighs.

"Oh!"

"I'd love you to read it," he said.

"Hmmmmm."

Alex continued speaking softly, in almost a whisper, about his screenplay while slipping his fingers inside her so slowly she hardly knew it was happening until all her attention was focused on his fingertips. Okay, it *was* about sex. The kind of highly verbal, intellectual sex that transpires between people who are aroused by metaphors.

The more sex Ruth had, the more she wanted. Not just with Alex but with Witty to whom she was now officially "engaged to be engaged." She knew in her heart that if she saw only Alex, they would self-combust in short order. Passion of this intensity always burns itself out. If she was faithful to Witty, they would soon fall into the familiar pattern of finishing each other's sentences and turning their backs on each other in bed. Ruth didn't feel divided. In fact, she had never felt so complete.

36

Larry had a lot to learn. The New York drag scene had changed. It wasn't just about wearing a wig, make-up and camping it up, lip-syncing to *Cats* anymore. It was truly *OUT THERE.* Wearing his Jackie-O ensemble, he sauntered into Barracuda for the weekly amateur drag show hosted by Sherika, a gorgeous, toilet-mouthed tranny with mocha skin and blond tendrils down to *there.*

Sipping a vodka gimlet, Larry observed the eclectic crowd of queens, gays, gawkers, trannies and bachelorettes. He would never subject himself to the humiliation of competing in a drag contest. And yet. He was fascinated by the beautiful young Asian cross-dressers, strutting with super model hauteur and singing *All the Single Ladies.* A Madonna clone with a ripped body came out in black leather chaps and did things with a bull whip to *Justify My Love.* They were kids, half Larry's age. They lived in another world. A world Larry found fresh, invigorating and fabulous. But a world in which there was no room for what Larry desired more than anything – passing for straight.

His next stop was Lucky Cheng's. The bartender was a 300-pound dyke. The waitresses were old queens. Larry felt there was something sad about an old queen, unless she looked like Barbara Walters, ready for her close up. Or better yet. Like Catherine Deneuve. Dignity. That's what Larry valued. And there was nothing dignified about a sixty-year old drag queen giving a lap dance to a straight but very drunk hedge fund manager.

"You look like you could use an orgy."

Larry turned in his seat at the bar.

"Don't worry. It's a drink, not an invitation," said a silver-haired businessman.

From his two-hundred dollar hair cut, Larry figured he was being picked up by an escapee from the Upper East Side. A man of means. Straight but curious.

"I'll accept the drink," Larry said, "But I'll tell you up front, I'm not *looking.*"

"I didn't think you were." He smiled and signaled the bartender for Larry's drink. "You're not dressed like Cher," Silver Fox continued. "I could take you to the bar at the St Regis and, if people stared, it would only be because you're stunning."

"Thank you," Larry said. "But I would never walk into the St. Regis dressed like this."

"Why the hell not?" Silver Fox asked.

"Because I haven't made the transition yet. I'm just, uh, trying it on for size."

Over a cocktail the size of an aquarium, Larry explained what he hadn't told anyone else. He had started taking hormones six months ago and would not be having gender re-assignment surgery until the following year. That is, if he could come up with the money.

"I'm between two worlds," he said. "It's quite precarious."

"I understand," said Silver Fox, gently resting a tanned, manicured hand on Larry's. "If you ever need someone to talk to, call me."

"I just might take you up on that," Larry said. "What about you? What's your story?"

"Nowhere near as interesting as yours." Silver Hair laughed. "I was married, two kids." *Surprise. Surprise.* "I love women. All women. Including women like you."

"But I'm not a woman. Not yet."

"You will be. And when you are…." He slid a business card in Larry's direction.

The card was engraved with a name Larry instantly recognized. It was an Old Money New York name, right up there with the Astors, Rockefellers and Vanderbilts. A name synonymous with hospital wings, art museums and Page Six. More thrillingly, it was the name of a boy Larry had secretly had a crush on at Dalton. One of those Golden Boys with sun-streaked hair and honeyed skin who "summered" in Bar Harbor and "wintered" in Palm Beach. Larry never had the nerve to speak to him when they were kids. Now here they were, practically holding hands in a gay bar. He doesn't know who I am, he thought. And neither do I.

"What exactly do you do?" Larry asked, pulling out a cigarette.

Silver Fox leaned in close and lit it.

"Whatever I want," He said, giving Larry a kiss on the cheek and sauntering out the door.

Larry took a second look at the card. It was embossed on thick, high quality stock. He twirled it between his fingers and smiled.

37

Some people are hoarders. Ruth had the opposite compulsion. Throwing things out – be they old coffee mugs, clothes or journals – energized her. She made a grand sweep of her childhood bedroom, tossing Barbies and stuffed animals into a large green plastic trash bag. Down came the Springstein poster, Matisse prints and rainbow banner. She opened a white leatherette jewelry box concealing a twirling plastic ballerina that played *Sunrise Sunset* and paused to examine peace-sign pendants, dolphin earrings and Swatch watches, before dumping them. Tugging open bureau drawers, Ruth passed swift judgment. *Out, out, out!*

"What are you doing?" cried Dolly, "What's inside all those bags?"

"Stuff I don't need anymore."

Dolly bent down, opened a bag and let out a yelp.

"You can't do this," Dolly said, cradling Kermit the Frog. "You have no right. These things belong to my daughter."

Ruth saw the tears brimming over in her mother's eyes, the trembling of her lip.

"I'm *not* throwing anything away," said Ruth who was looking forward to heaving the bag down the trash chute. "I'm just putting them in storage, where they'll be safe."

"Storage?" Dolly said doubtfully.

"In the basement."

Dolly turned and shuffled away, clutching Kermit. She wasn't lifting her feet when she walked anymore. Pushing one foot flatly ahead of the other, Dolly made a pathetic *shush-shush* sound with every step.

After dumping the remnants of her teenaged self down the chute, Ruth tackled her father's closet. Months after his funeral, it was still filled with monogrammed shirts, Brooks Brother suits and Bally shoes. Ruth pressed her face against a cable knit cardigan sweater and breathed in her father's scent. Old English Leather and Juicy Fruit. His clothes were too new to toss. She would offer them to Geneva, perhaps she knew of a family member or church that would welcome them.

"What are you doing with Daddy's clothes?"

"They're just going to waste," Ruth said and immediately regretted it as she watched the confusion in her mother's eyes.

"GET OUT! GET OUT!" Dolly yelled, grabbing a suit jacket out of Ruth's hands.

This angry old woman was *not* her mother. She was one in a succession of increasingly unsociable beings who were inhabiting her mother's brain. Dolly had always been talkative, a veritable chatterbox. Now she sat staring into her lap, while people spoke around and over her like a child. Her eyes had lost their sparkle, her lips sometimes moved silently, her body slumped over upon itself.

Long before Dolly had shown any signs of aging, she had made her wishes clear. "I don't want to be a vegetable," she said. "I don't want to be a burden on my children."

Larry and Naomi interpreted this to mean that their mother did not want *them* to suffer. Ruth took them literally. When Dolly said "vegetable," Ruth conjured up a giant zucchini in a hospital gown. When she said "burden," Ruth imagined herself carrying her mother around in a burlap sack on her back while going about her daily routine, stopping off at Starbucks, going to the dry cleaner. Although Dolly was in no condition to either remember or enforce her final wishes, Ruth felt it was her duty to honor them and, in that regard, she was stockpiling pills – Ambien, Xanax, Co-Tylenol – for the day when Dolly's quality of life was over. But that day was a constantly moving target. When Mom becomes incontinent. When Mom's in a wheelchair. When she can't feed herself. With each setback, Ruth said to herself, "Soon, soon, but not yet."

Ruth's pledge was a double-edged sword. If she "helped" her mother end her life, her siblings would accuse her of murder. If she didn't, she'd be betraying a sacred trust. Dolly would suffer. And so Ruth prayed, guiltily, for her mother's speedy and painless death. To relieve the guilt, she attempted to maintain a veneer of normality for Dolly. Ruth styled her mother's hair, tweezed her brows and odd hairs sprouting on her cheeks and chin, reminded her to put on lipstick and bought her new clothes to replace the ones that were stained. She escorted Dolly to the park, the corner coffee shop, museums, the ballet and concerts until it became evident that these excursions created more anxiety than pleasure for her mother. All the while, acutely aware that strangers, especially the elderly, stared at Dolly, not in pity, but in dread.

Ruth was unaware that the energy with which she redecorated her bedroom, painting its walls a pale gray and replacing the frilly bedspread with a slate linen duvet from ABC, was driven by fear. Caring for a mother with dementia gave Ruth a front row seat in a drama few can watch without turning to drink, sex or religion. Ruth was not a boozer or a believer. That left only one option.

38

"When did you decide to become a television writer?" Alex asked.

"After I failed at everything else," Ruth said.

He was at the stove frying up a zucchini and cheddar frittata in a cast-iron skillet. Ruth sat at the kitchen table, dipping whole grain bread into olive oil seasoned with cilantro and cayenne pepper. After sex, they were always famished. Ruth, for food. Alex, for shop talk. Although she was still sloshing about in afterglow and reluctant to discuss anything that would pull her back to reality, Ruth complied.

"I was a theatre major in college." she said. "When I graduated, I took the usual route. Waitressing at night and making the rounds of auditions during the day. It didn't take long to realize that if I couldn't memorize the Specials of the Day, I'd never get through *Long Days Journey into Night*."

"So you went from acting to writing?" He slid a wedge of frittata onto Ruth's plate.

"Not directly. I briefly worked at my father's dress company. Then for a caterer, an interior designer and Tower Records. No matter what I did, they always said the same thing. You're not a team player."

Alex scooped golden wedges of frittata onto cobalt plates and joined her at the table. Ruth took a mouthful, made appreciative noises, then proceeded to talk and eat at the same time, a habit considered gauche in some circles but a survival skill within her culture. If Jews didn't talk and eat at the same time, her father was fond of saying, it would've taken four *hundred* years, not forty, to cross the dessert.

"Eventually, I enrolled in a writing course at the New School. I had a great instructor and found my voice, as they say. It had been there all along but it hadn't occurred to me that I could make a career of it, that anyone would pay me to, well, be who I am."

"Yes. Yes. That's it, exactly," Alex said, slapping his palm on the table, making the plates dance. "That's what being a writer is about. To be who you *are*."

"Or to be James Patterson."

Alex didn't blink.

"So how did you get your start in LA?" he prodded. "Did you have contacts there? Friends or relatives in the business?"

Ruth was growing bored with this conversation. These were the same questions she got from students when she taught Introduction to Television Writing at UCLA Extension. She was more interested in Alex's life than her own. Why had his marriage ended? Did he have an affair or did she? Was he still in love with her? On the other hand, Ruth was well aware that her career, as marginal as it was these days, was what made her exciting to Alex.

"I didn't know anyone in LA," Ruth said. "My first job was at Disney, answering phones for development executives. This was before cell phones and email. There was this whole S&M ritual about getting people on the phone. People got their rocks off *not* returning calls. No one, but no one, took calls during the day. It was a sign of power even if they were asleep at their desk. So I took messages on little pink slips all day long and at the Golden Hour, between six and seven p.m., they would return calls in order of importance."

"Sounds boring," Alex said.

"Oh, it was. If I had thought of it is as real job, I wouldn't have lasted a week. But my goal wasn't to sit on Michael Eisner's lap. It was to learn the business. Development execs don't read screenplays. They *could* but they consider it beneath them. That's what I did when I wasn't taking messages. I read scripts and turned them into one-page summaries called coverage. It was like being the member of a secret firing squad. If I checked one box, the screenwriter could be catapulted into a Malibu beach house. If I checked another, he'd have to hold onto his day job at Bed, Bath and Beyond.

"They give all that power to the lowest person in the chain?" Alex asked.

"Scary, huh? But it helped me understand why good scripts go bad and how to fix them. I continued answering phones and taking lunch orders for production companies for a couple of years before I sold my first screenplay."

"Who starred in it?"

"Nobody. It was never produced. Scripts are Hollywood junk bonds. They get bought, sold, traded, purely on speculation and hubris.

Alex cleared the plates and led Ruth by the hand back to the bedroom. He lit up a cigarillo and put on that damn tango music. *Maybe if I buy him some Segovia he'll get the hint. And those cigars.* She nestled against him, laying her head over his chest so she could hear his heart thud.

"Who's your agent?" he whispered into her hair.

"Um, Aloha Weinberg. Can you open a window?"

"Do you like her?" His fingers lightly strummed her nipples.

Aloha had stopped returning her calls months ago. The mention of her name made Ruth want to reach for a Xanax. Instead, she grasped Alex's cock.

"She's okay, I guess."

"How long have you been with her?"

Ruth climbed on top of him.

"Oh, I don't know," she said, feeling him harden. "Six years. Maybe seven."

Alex tossed his cigarillo into an ashtray and placed his hands on her hips, setting the pace. An agonizingly slow tango as opposed to the frantic salsa of their earlier lovemaking.

"Does she only represent television writers or screenwriters too?"

He lifted her, held her there, hovering. *Ohhhhhhhhhh.* Then filled her again and again.

"YES. YES. Screenwriters too! OH. YES!"

39

"So you got yourself a fuck monkey," said Gabby Lee.

"I beg your pardon?" Ruth said.

"Oh, don't look at me like that. You know what I'm talking about. A boy toy? A stud muffin? A vibrator that leaves the toilet seat up?"

Ruth was horrified. She had a burning need to tell someone about her affair with Alex. (What good is a secret relationship if nobody knows?) Gabby seemed to be the ideal candidate. She was worldly, non-judgmental and didn't know anyone in Ruth's small circle. But here she was, turning Ruth's romantic trysts into a crude joke.

"It's not just about sex," Ruth explained. "Alex is a published writer. He's highly intelligent. We have incredible conversations that go on and on for hours."

"Where? At the public library? Or in bed?" Gabby snickered.

"Well...."

"And he's hung like Sea Biscuit. Am I right?"

Gabby was right. But Ruth wasn't about to acknowledge the remark.

"There's nothing better for a woman's complexion than fresh sperm," Gabby said. "Why do you think women start wrinkling when they turn fifty? It's cause they've run out of the damn stuff. Their husbands are busy clearing the complexions of lap dancers."

Gabby Lee was on her fourth glass of pink champagne. It was two o'clock in the morning and she was just revving up. Eduardo brought in a tray of miniature hot dogs with a side dish of spicy mustard.

"There isn't a caterer in Manhattan who can come up with a better appetizer," said Gabby, popping one into her mouth, then making Ike and Tina beg for treats. "All these hoity-toity society affairs where they serve steak tartar and lamb's tongue? You give 'em weiners, there'll be a stampede."

Ruth grabbed a toothpick and stabbed a hot dog.

"You're not drinking," Gabby noted. "You're not pregnant, are you?"

"God, no."

"So many of my writers get pregnant, I think it's from sitting on that sofa. It saw a lot of action in its day."

Ruth shifted.

"Don't worry. It's been reupholstered," Gabby said. "So, tell me, you still seeing the other guy?"

"Yes. They're very different. I don't think I could be happy with either one. But with both, it's perfect."

"Smart girl," Gabby said. "Every woman needs a man with deep pockets *and* a man with big balls. The old yin and yang."

Ruth had a feeling this is not what Buddha had in mind when he described the oppositional forces of the universe.

"That's why I didn't divorce Mel when I found out why it took him four hours to walk the dogs in Central Park. He was my best friend and a brilliant business manager. But being loved wasn't enough. I wanted to be *desired.* So I got myself a fuck monkey. Cute. Young. Hung. Not terribly bright."

Why was Gabby telling her this? Her sordid affairs had nothing in common with Ruth's cerebral relationship with Alex. Gabby had the face of a forty-year-old in a wind tunnel and a body that clearly signaled all the infirmities of old age. Stooped posture, arthritic hands, leathery skin. *Christ, she's as old my mother and she's talking about male genitalia.*

"Of course, I never keep them for long unless they have *other* talents," Gabby said, rolling her eyes toward Eduardo. When he left the room, she confided, "He's an excellent cook. Sarah Jessica Parker tried to steal him away but I made him an offer he couldn't refuse. I gave him a Rolls."

It was the time of night when Ruth wondered what she was doing at Gabby Lee's and longed for the simple comforts of her own messy bed and a bag of Double Chocolate Milanos. And yet Gabby had a way of drawing her in, of dangling the promise of the keys to the Enchanted Kingdom. *She knows people. She could help me get a real job. Writing for Letterman or Leno. All I have to do is play along.* Ike and Tina jumped on Ruth's lap, feverish for attention. She didn't hate dogs. She just hated Ike and Tina. They were avid crotch-sniffers, an experience Ruth rated right up there with being groped on the subway.

"I'm so glad you love my puppies," Gabby said. "I want you to mention them regularly in the filler."

"Will do," Ruth said.

"Great. Come over at 4 o'clock tomorrow afternoon and Eduardo will have them ready."

"Um. I don't understand. What exactly do you want me to do?" Ruth said.

"Get to know Ike and Tina's personalities. Take them to the park, go to that adorable doggie couture shop on Madison, have *fun* with them."

Ruth paled. She had just been demoted to dog walker.

40

It was a glorious spring day. Ike and Tina trotted happily up 79th Street toward Central Park, stopping to inspect every tree and turd along the way. People smiled at Ruth, which is normally considered a sign of insanity in New York unless one has an adorable child or pooch in tow. They stopped to ask the dogs' names and to marvel at their tiny Burberry coats. Some had dogs of their own that danced wildly at the end of their leashes in anticipation of the orgy of rectal sniffing that occasions canine introductions. A few brave souls leaned over to pet Ike and Tina. Ruth feared for their fingers. But the mutts rolled over on their backs begging for belly rubs. One of these dog-obsessed strangers was a handsome man who was so enraptured by Ike and Tina that he pulled out his cell phone and took their photo.

"Pomeranians are the *best*," he said. "I've got two at home."

Ruth had once dated a man who shared his bed with a German Shepherd. Once was more than enough. She tugged Ike and Tina's leashes, steering them across Fifth Avenue. As soon as they entered the park, the dogs' gait accelerated from a dainty trot to a frenzied gallop, pulling Ruth along in their wake. She had to run to keep up.

"Whoa, guys, whoa!" she hollered.

People on park benches smiled thinking Ruth was out for a healthy run with her furry companions, not seeing the panic in her eyes. *This is ridiculous. They're just little dogs. I'm in control.* She dug in her heels and pulled back hard on their leads, sending Ike and Tina flying straight up into the air. They landed on the macadam path, whimpering pathetically.

"Oh, my god," cried an elderly woman, leaning over the yelping pups.

"That's animal abuse," said a tattooed kid on a skateboard, whipping out his cell phone to document the incident.

"Lady, you ought to be ashamed of yourself," admonished a man in a white linen suit and red bow tie.

"I'm sorry. I'm sorry," Ruth wailed. "They aren't mine."

"Thank God," smirked a young woman clutching what looked like a furry rat to her breast.

Tiny dogs with bulging eyes, the uglier the better, had become a fashion accessory. Ruth did her best to demonstrate that she was not a sadistic monster, bending down to talk to Ike and Tina in cooing tones. Ike smiled and sank his teeth into her hand.

"OUCH!" Ruth yelped.

"You deserved it, Lady," said the guy in the white suit.

Blood dripped from her hand. This was too much. As Ruth dug into her purse for a tissue, Ike and Tina seized the moment to pursue lunch in the form of an unsuspecting squirrel. When she looked up they were streaking across the meadow toward Turtle Lake, a final repository for pet turtles who had out-lived their owner's affections. *Good. Let them drown.* Then Ruth pictured Gabby's face melting into a mask of tragedy, in as much as her cosmetically paralyzed muscles would allow.

Ruth trekked across the grassy meadow, stepping gingerly over dog poop, used condoms and plastic gloves, the flotsam and jetsam of a city park. She gave wide berth to people lying on the grass, on blankets and on each other. Some couples provided a romantic tableau of Young Love. Checkered tablecloth, wicker basket, wine and cheese. Others, with pants unzipped and skirts hiked to the waist, appeared to be engaged in the world's oldest profession *en plein air.*

* * * *

Ike and Tina paddled furiously about the lake, smiles on their pointy little faces, daring Ruth to come and get them. As a child, she had pulled the same stunt, gleefully jumping waves at Jones Beach while her mother frantically beckoned from the shore. You're turning blue, Dolly would holler to no avail. What six-year-old doesn't want to turn blue? Or purple, for that matter. Ruth knew her mother wouldn't wade in deeper than her knees. God forbid she should get her Gottex suit wet. Similarly, Ruth had no intention of taking off her green suede Arche shoes and ruining her Ann Taylor linen slacks. Supposedly, there were hundreds, perhaps thousands, of turtles just beneath the lake's mirror surface. The thought of stepping on one… UGH!

"Hey, lady. You want your dogs? I can get 'em for ten bucks," asked a kid wearing a METS cap.

Ruth hesitated. He looked to be around ten years old. She wasn't sure how deep the lake was. Suppose he drowned? That would be harder to explain than losing the dogs.

"Can you swim?" she asked.

The kid wrinkled his face and nodded, but instead of jumping into the lake he whistled and threw a broken tree branch towards the aquatic canines. Ike grabbed the branch in his mouth, swam to shore and dropped it at the boy's feet. Tina was right behind, shaking herself wildly, spraying water in every direction. Ruth only had twenties in her wallet and the kid didn't have change or, if he did, wasn't about to forfeit an easy profit.

Soaking wet, covered in pond slime, Ike and Tina did not attract admirers on the way home. Ruth fully expected Gabby to fire her on the spot, not just as a dog walker but as her writer. And report her for animal cruelty. God knows, Ruth had lost jobs for less.

Gabby, however, found Ruth's misadventure in the park to be "hysterical."

"Make it sexy," Gabby instructed. "Instead of a kid, make it a hunky guy who strips off his shirt and pants. You get the picture?"

Ruth got it.

41

Sol stood naked at the bedroom window scratching his behind.

"For God's sake. Put some clothes on. You're on display," admonished Dolly.

"Who's looking? The pigeons?"

"People in other buildings can see."

"So let them catch some pleasure," he said, flexing his biceps.

The sex machine she had married still thought of himself as an Adonis. He came over to the vanity where she was brushing her hair, slipped a hand under her robe and squeezed a breast.

"Sol!"

"Aw, c'mon. It's Saturday."

Dolly batted him away with her hairbrush.

"Tonight," she said. "When the children are sleeping."

That was another thing. Dolly, an innately modest woman, preferred sex in the dark, while Sol woke up every morning at full mast. Before the kids, he could coax her into a morning quickie. Now, he had to take matters into his own hands. The sad truth was that Sol loved making babies but raising them was a different story. The birth of each of his children had created yet another obstacle to having Dolly all to himself. Naomi was a whiner. Ruth had such a mouth on her. And Larry was a little tyrant, never satisfied, always demanding *more*. Reluctantly, he put on a pair of striped boxer shorts and followed Dolly to the kitchen.

"Mother's coming today," she said, putting up the coffee.

"What for?"

"To watch the girls while I take Larry to a specialist."

"Another one?" Sol groaned. "Why not just donate him to science?"

"Sol! He'll hear you."

"I'm just saying, maybe all that's wrong with him is these *fahrkakte* doctors. If you'd just leave him be, he'd… adjust."

"Larry takes after me. He's sensitive. Did I tell you he was voted president of the Dalton Drama Club?"

"I'm not surprised. He's a regular Sarah Bernhardt."

Dolly slammed a drawer shut. Her hands were shaking. She did not lose her temper easily or often, but when it came to her children, she was a lioness.

"Listen, Sol, when I was Larry's age, I had all the leading roles at the Neighborhood Center. The director wrote me a recommendation for the Actor's Studio. But I met a fast-talking guy who promised me the moon and the stars."

Sol took Dolly's hand. He had heard this story many times.

"And did I deliver?" he asked.

"The moon? Yes. The stars? I'm still waiting."

She placed a cup of coffee, a small glass of orange juice and a toasted sesame bagel with cream cheese on a plastic placemat in front of Sol. She remained standing like a waitress.

"So who you taking him to this time?" Sol asked.

"Dr. Malik, a top endocrinologist on Park Avenue. They think it could be something hormonal."

"Park Avenue, huh? I'll tell you one thing, it's going to be something expensive." He waved his hand before Dolly could respond. "But when it comes to the children's health...."

Sol pulled Dolly onto his lap and kissed her full on the mouth. When the doorbell rang, she squirmed out of his grasp, retying her robe.

"That must be Mother," she said, calling out, "I'm coming. I'm coming."

It wasn't Mother. It was a girl with a nose ring. Something about her looked vaguely familiar. A new neighbor perhaps?

"Yes?" said Dolly.

"Hello, Grandma," replied Shoshanna.

"You must have the wrong apartment," Dolly said.

"It's okay, Mom," Ruth shouted from the hall. "It's Shoshanna."

Dolly looked in confusion at the stranger. Her granddaughter Shoshanna was an adorable little child, not a *mishugana* with rings in her nose.

"I'm going to watch my program," Dolly announced, tottering back to the den.

"Don't take it personally," Ruth said to her niece. "This isn't one of her good days."

"That makes two of us," Shoshanna sighed, putting her Doc Martins up on the custom made sofa as only someone who has never paid for one can do.

Ruth didn't say anything. Her niece's visits were a godsend.

"My parents are so fucked," Shoshanna said. "Their threatening to stop paying for my dorm room."

Ruth usually let her niece vent without taking sides. But this sounded serious.

"Why?" Ruth asked.

"They're pissed because I stopped going to class."

"Oh?"

"I want to be a fashion designer not a fucking seamstress," she wailed. "I don't want to learn how to sew."

"How many classes have you missed?"

"All of them," Shoshanna mumbled.

"You never went to a single class this term?"

"What's the big deal? I got all the money back from the registrar. They didn't want to give it to me but I wouldn't leave the office until I got every fucking dollar."

"Wait. I'm confused," Ruth said. "You got a full refund on your tuition? And you're still living in the dorm?"

"Yeh. So?"

Ruth wasn't sure she wanted to venture any further into her niece's convoluted thinking but couldn't resist.

"You gave the refund to your parents?"

"Fuck no," Shoshanna said. "That's *my* money."

"Your money? You earned it?"

Shoshanna twirled her hair with her fingers.

"Yeh. By being Naomi and Howard Karp's child for eighteen fucking years."

Entitlement issues. Must be in the water.

"So what are you going to do now?" Ruth asked, as casually as possible, afraid that her niece was planning on moving into the El Coronado.

"I'm going to work for a caterer. Very high end. The pay is awesome."

Ruth wasn't about to inquire into her niece's experience in the food service industry which, as far she knew, was limited to selling Girl Scout Cookies.

"Good for you," Ruth said as if Shoshanna were embarking on a MBA at Harvard. "Are you going to be here for a while? I need to run out for an hour."

* * * *

Alex tugged down the zipper of Ruth's jeans with his teeth and was in the process of licking off her panties when she stopped him.

"Let's go to the park," she said.

"Now?" he said from between her legs.

"It's a beautiful day. We can spread out on a blanket. Have a picnic."

"I *am* having a picnic."

"But we never go out," she said, squirming away from his voracious mouth. "It would be fun. Exciting."

Alex stood up and scratched his head, then grabbed two throw pillows and a tablecloth.

"Ok," he said, leading Ruth by the hand. "C'mon."

He slid open the door leading to the backyard, flung down the tablecloth and pillows and stripped off his shirt and jeans.

"What are you doing?" she said.

"Honoring your request."

"But...but your neighbors. They can *see*."

"Lucky for them."

42

"A friend's coming for dinner tonight," Larry announced on a drizzly April afternoon. "I'd appreciate it if you'd keep mother out of the living and dining room."

Ruth didn't know what surprised her more. That Larry was cooking or that he had a friend.

"This is a very important evening for me," he said. "I don't want any disruptions. The food will arrive from Café Outre around six o'clock. My guest at eight."

So much for Larry's culinary skills. Café Outre was a French Moroccan bistro that served peasant food at sultan prices. Ruth was dying to know the identity of his guest but she could tell from the tap tap tapping of his foot that he was not in sharing mode.

"Fine," she said. "You won't even know we're here."

* * * *

Ruth picked up cheeseburgers and fries at the Greek coffee shop on the corner and ate with her mother in the den while Vanna White turned letters.

"The early bird catches the worm!" Dolly shouted, solving the puzzle before the contestant and vicariously winning five hundred dollars.

Dolly's now-you-see-it-now-you-don't mental acuity was a subject of fascination for Ruth. Every display of her intellect was proof. Mom was still Mom. Dolly made short work of her burger and attacked the fries with vigor. Her food preferences seemed to have regressed along with her memory. At one time a connoisseur of fine dining, Dolly now craved the salty, sweet foods of a teenaged pothead. She would subsist exclusively on donuts, ice cream and potato chips if Ruth permitted. And at this point, why not? High cholesterol was no longer the boogie man. Death by stoke would be a godsend.

Later, with Dolly down for the night, Ruth climbed into bed and started to read Alex's screenplay *Naked Conversations.* She didn't like the title but titles are always changed. She tapped a red pen against her teeth, prepared to write the usual banal remarks. *Nice! Less is more! Show - don't tell!* But she had flown past page ten – the most critical pages of any script - without making a mark. The premise was Alex's own story of a turbulent marriage to an emotionally unstable Italian heiress, told from the point of view of the couple's five-year-old son. The dialogue, pacing and character development were on the money. Okay, she told herself, he's a talented writer and probably took one of those screenwriter's boot camp workshops. But he's going to hit a wall and go off-track in the second act. All first-time screenwriters do.

Ruth reached the last page; her heart was racing. The ending, which most novice writers drag out too long, was deftly handled. When the wife goes back to Italy, the distraught protagonist temporarily experiences writers block and then, by chance, sees his future in the smile of a woman he meets in a café. *Me! This is why he wanted me to read it. His screenplay expresses what he hasn't had the courage to say!*

43

"What's new?" Dolly asked Ruth ten times a day.

In the beginning, Ruth replied, "Nothing," and watched as disappointment clouded her mother's eyes. Now Ruth employed a new tactic. She told Dolly the truth, describing in detail her relationship with Witty, her affair with Alex and her work with Gabby Lee. These confessionals were highly entertaining for Dolly. For Ruth, they were cathartic. Free therapy sessions in which Dolly provided as much support as any psychologist. Trust your feelings, she said. Don't take shit from anyone, she said. Occasionally, Dolly appeared to nod off, but then so had Ruth's therapist. It was to her mother that Ruth brought her romantic problems, knowing it would go no further because dementia wiped Dolly's mental slate clean every few minutes.

"I'm not in love with Witty," Ruth said.

"Love *schmov*," Dolly shrugged. "How does he treat you? Is he kind? Caring? Does he make a living?"

"Yes. Yes. Yes. But there's someone else."

"Have I met him?"

"Uh, no." Ruth looked down into her lap.

"What? You're ashamed of your mother?"

"No. No. It's just that, well, I usually go to *his* place."

Dolly's eyes narrowed.

"He doesn't take you *out*?"

"I know it sounds bad but, Mom, I'm *crazy* about him."

Dolly let out a sigh long enough to deflate a Goodyear tire.

"Life is short but a bad marriage can make you wish it was even shorter." Dolly cupped Ruth's face in her hands. "Don't rush into anything."

Five minutes from now, Dolly would not remember this conversation. But Ruth would. She marveled at her mother's in-the-moment clarity and something else that had always been there. Her unconditional love.

* * * *

"She won't let me change her clothes," Geneva said.

Dolly had been a fastidious dresser but was becoming increasingly resistant to efforts to keep her in fresh clothes, often insisting on wearing the same outfit two days running. Today, Dolly was wearing a white blouse with a large tomato soup stain shaped like the state of Florida. At the sight of Ruth, she brightened and stretched out her arms.

"Thank God, you're here. You have no idea what's been going on," Dolly said.

"What's going on, Mom?"

Dolly looked towards the door.

"The nurse is trying to steal my clothes," she whispered.

"Mom, she's not a nurse. It's Geneva. The housekeeper."

"Geneva? I remember Geneva. What ever happened to her?"

"She's here. Why don't you put on something nice and we'll have lunch with her?"

"I don't have anything to wear. The nurse stole all my clothes." Dolly was near tears.

This was another of Dolly's new themes. People were stealing. In most cases, the missing object was within plain sight or could be easily located. Other times, things appeared where least expected. A bra in the freezer. Shoes in the dishwasher. When pieces of Daum crystal and other valuables started to disappear, Geneva expressed concern, not wanting anyone to accuse her of stealing.

"See? All your clothes are here," Ruth said, opening her mother's closet.

Dolly clapped her hands with joy.

"Do you want to wear the lavender print or the blue outfit?" Ruth asked.

Rather than asking Dolly what she wanted to wear, which would've overwhelmed her, or insisting she wear a particular outfit, Ruth gave her mother a choice.

"I think the blue is better," Dolly said.

Placidly, Dolly allowed Ruth to unbutton and remove the stained blouse, unhook her bra, take off her underpants and put on fresh clothes. It was like dressing a life-size doll. But sometimes, Dolly shouted "get the hell away from me" and drove Ruth to tears. Dolly's moments of mental acuity were more startling than her shroud of confusion. She still looked at the newspaper every day and recited the headlines out loud, but there was no telling her level of comprehension. When a *New York Times* headline screamed SUICIDE BOMBER STRIKES AGAIN, Ruth was quick to explain.

"It happened in Iraq, Mom. On the other side of the world. The President declared war and sent U.S. soldiers there," Ruth said.

"Easy for him to do, sitting in the White House, sending young boys off to die."

173

If this was dementia - what was sanity?

Still. Much of what Dolly said and did was nonsensical. She insisted on carrying her handbag at all times, even when she was going no further than the kitchen and she accused the neighbors of stealing her dog. The one that died twenty years ago.

"You're just like a daughter to me," Dolly said to Ruth.

"Mom, I *am* your daughter."

"Oh, thank God!"

This exchange occurred every day. And so the simple, humbling act of helping her mother took on special, almost Biblical, meaning for Ruth. Getting Dolly into the shower was a nightmare. She had developed a fear of water which, Ruth learned, was a common symptom of dementia. It was counterintuitive. How could a woman who never missed her weekly beauty salon appointment suddenly refuse to have her hair washed? But that's exactly what Dolly did, loudly and emphatically, in front of the flustered salon owner, leaving no choice but to wash her hair at home with dry shampoo. This was yet another task with which Ruth had more success than Geneva.

Rather than resent her mother's increasing dependence, Ruth felt it was the natural order of things. Babies are incontinent, they babble incoherently, and can't dress or bathe themselves, but they aren't shipped off to nursing homes, she argued. To which Larry replied, "But babies are *cute*. And they grow up."

The only one who truly understood was Mr. Greenbaum. His late wife had Alzheimer's. When Ruth expressed her exasperation with Dolly's habit of drifting from the present to the past, Greenbaum corrected her.

"Your mother's not lost," he said. "She's just commuting."

44

"Larry, what is this?" Ruth asked, opening a small envelop.

"Tickets for the Andrea Bocelli concert at Lincoln Center this afternoon. I thought mother would enjoy getting out and it would be a nice break for you and Geneva."

Ruth had been making an effort to take Dolly to hear live music and see films, but lately, her mother's attention wandered and a short walk to the park was all she could manage.

"It's very thoughtful of you but I think it might be too much for her," Ruth said.

"Nonsense. Geneva will be with you. Take a cab," he said, handing Ruth two twenties.

"You're not coming with us?" she asked.

"No, no. I have work to do."

Larry's "work" was a mystery. He said he was doing something for a law firm but he never left the apartment until after dark. Ruth didn't trust him but couldn't think of a reason to turn down his offer. As she steered Dolly out the door, Larry called after them.

"Take my cell phone number and call me before you come back. I'll order take-out Chinese for dinner and it will be ready when you arrive," he said.

Ruth said "great" but threw Geneva a meaningful glance. Larry always went out for dinner, never saying where he was going or when he would return. Since the start of Dolly's illness, he hadn't once offered to help with shopping or preparing meals. That didn't stop him from invading the kitchen at odd hours, leaving dirty dishes in the sink and a chicken carcass picked clean of meat in the fridge. When the elevator door closed, Geneva sighed, "The Lord works in wondrous ways."

Larry bolted the door shut. He put Mahler's Eighth Symphony on his CD player, turned up the volume and conducted a search and seizure mission that would've brought tears to the eyes of Navy Seals. Clandestine operations were nothing new to Larry who had been raiding his mother's and sisters' closets since he was in kindergarten. To have the entire apartment to himself was thrilling.

His father had kept important papers in a vault at Chase Manhattan which Larry had emptied. But his mother hid things "for safe keeping" in the apartment and, invariably, forgot where they were, even before her illness. He started with her bedroom, leaving no drawer, handbag or shoebox unopened. The scent of her closet, an amalgam of perfume, fur and camphor, brought back a flood of memories. Trying on Mommy's shoes and pearls when he was four years old, wandering into the dining room where she was playing mahjong and having all the beautiful ladies make such a fuss over him, picking him up, covering his face with lipstick kisses.

When Larry was in his early teens, his mother's clothes fit him perfectly, but after he shot up to 6'2," he had to content himself with just her makeup and accessories. Scarves, belts, jewelry, handbags. Dolly had an impressive collection of Italian alligator bags, all purchased at Saks. Larry opened each one, marveling at their good condition, the delicious "snap" of the metal fasteners and the quality of the stitching. They were highly collectible, worth ten times what his mother paid for them, and going to waste in her closet. She wouldn't need a vintage Gucci purse where she was going. The closet yielded up no secrets other than a shoebox filled with tissue-thin letters from someone named Frank. At the bottom of a bureau drawer, underneath bras, panties and slips, Larry found a scrapbook containing every letter and photo he had sent his mother from Amsterdam. He was tempted to read the letters, but it would have to wait.

Going through Dolly's jewelry, Larry made a mental note to put it in a safety box in yet another bank. Dolly no longer needed gold bangles or diamond bracelets and he couldn't imagine either of his sisters wearing a strand of perfect pearls. Sitting at his mother's mirrored vanity where he had primped and posed for hours as a boy, Larry put on her lipstick and sprayed Chanel No. 5 on his neck. As he twirled around on the swivel chair, his eyes fell on the king-sized bed. Of course. It's so obvious. He threw back the bedspread, blankets and sheets and stuck his hands under the mattress all around the edges. At the lower corner, on his mother's side of the bed, he felt the sharp edge of an envelope. Inside were four-pages, stapled, The Last Will of Delores Sheraton, dated October 10, 2010, one week after Sol died.

"Being of sound mind...." *HAH!* "Hereby doth bequeath..." Blah, blah, blah. Larry read on, his lips moving, his heart pounding. His mother was leaving everything, but *everything*, including the apartment, to her "devoted daughter Ruth."

"I don't think so," Larry mused.

178

45

"The law is kind of squirrelly when it comes to dementia," said Tory over blue martinis at a Polynesian-themed lounge in Chelsea. "The individual isn't required to remember what they did or said in the past, only what they agree to in the immediate present."

"So no matter how mentally incompetent my mother is, she can still change her will?"

"As often as she wants. As long as there are witnesses or until she is declared incompetent and thomeone takes guardianthip."

Larry stared into the flame of the pupu platter, wondering how he would come up with two people to witness his mother's next and final will. Naomi and Ruth were out of the question.

"It's kind of ironic," Tory said. "People with dementia can vote. Which might explain the way things are going."

Larry smiled amicably. In Amsterdam, trashing American politics was a national pastime. Now that he was back in the States, he walked on eggshells, especially with Tory. Her work as a sexual discrimination lawyer put her in the liberal camp, but her family tree, alcohol consumption and wicked backhand hinted at Republican sympathies. Larry didn't give a shit about Tory's politics or religion. He would've gladly spoken in tongues if it would have given him a job at her firm.

For months now, she had thrown small amounts of work his way, legal briefs he could – and did – do in his sleep. But these weekly, alcohol-infused dinners weren't producing the results Larry wanted. Tory had yet to introduce him to her partners or offer a full time position, other than vague hints about how over-worked they were. Watching her lick her plump, greasy, fingers, he thought, what does Tory *really* want? That's when it finally dawned on Larry that the stocky, androgynous lawyer sitting across from him wanted to be *loved.*

"Are you seeing anyone special?" he asked.

"Like *when*?" she growled. "I work 24/7. I'm lucky to thee my parents on weekends. Christ, if I wanted a relationship, it would have to be with the FedEx guy."

She said *guy*, not gal.

"Let's say you had the time," Larry probed. "Describe your ideal mate."

Tory dipped another egg roll into the duck sauce.

"Well, he'd be a tiger in bed, Andre Agathi on the tennis court and Mario Batali in the kitchen. As if."

Larry was no Agasi but had never gotten any complaints in bed and, if pressed, he could make a damn good omelet. As they left the Blue Lagoon, he took Tory's hand.

"Why don't we have dinner at my place next week?" he said.

* * * *

Tory knew the El Coronado. It was impossible to live in Manhattan and not know it, with its Byzantine twin towers piercing the skyline of Central Park West. When she and Larry were schoolmates at Dalton, they hung out at Tory's house on the Upper East Side. Back then, Larry was embarrassed by the El Coronado. It was too *nouveau riche,* too Jewish. He preferred the more understated style of Tory's parent's east side brownstone with its worn Stickley furniture, faded cushions and Old Money smell. Tory's family had long ago sold their house on east 81ˢᵗ and lived alternately in Newport and Palm Beach, depending on the season. Tory's condo, which Larry had glimpsed just briefly, was a claustrophobic, Manhattan one-bedroom, suitable for sleeping, not living.

When Larry and Tory arrived, Dolly and Geneva were watching *Wheel of Fortune.*

"Mother, you remember Tory Van Hooten, my friend from Dalton?"

Dolly's mouth opened, nothing came out. She didn't remember what she had for lunch. Larry refused to alter the way he spoke to his mother, in spite of Ruth's urgings to be "sensitive." She remembers what she *wants* to remember, he insisted.

"Lovely to meet you," Dolly said, extending her hand.

"And this is Geneva, mother's…." said Larry.

"Companion," said Geneva evenly.

"Nice to meet you," said Tory.

"Your mother is charming. You would never know…," Tory said as Larry led her toward the dining room.

"This is one of her *good* days," he said in an undertone. "She really needs a higher level of care. My sister Ruth insists she can handle it herself. But, I ask you? Where is she?"

It was a rhetorical question which Larry could well have answered since he had instructed his sister to stay out of the apartment that night.

"A soon as Mother's *settled,* I'm going to re-do the whole place. It has so much potential."

"Will your thister continue to live here?" she asked.

"Good heavens, no," Larry snorted. "She has a home. In LA."

Tory wanted to rotate her fist in the air and make barking noises. She had always thought that the Sheraton's condo was more glamorous than the dull, drafty home in which she was raised. If Larry was making it his home, she would be spending more time here. Perhaps a *lot* more time.

"Thomething thmells delicious," Tory said as Larry steered her to the dining room.

"Nothing fussy, just a rack of lamb," he said, holding out her chair.

Truer words had never been spoken. Larry had dispensed with the "fuss" by hiring a personal chef to prepare gazpacho, herbed baby lamb chops, pan roasted potatoes and glazed carrots. Dessert was chocolate sorbet with fresh raspberries. A meal simple enough that one could imagine Larry pulling it off on his own, that is, if one didn't know Larry. The caterer had left a half hour before Tory arrived. All Larry had to do was pour the wine, a pinot noir and smile graciously when Tory swooned over the juicy pink chops and crispy potatoes.

"Oh, Larry, you've been holding out on me," she said.

In more ways than you can imagine. Inviting Tory to the apartment was a tactical move. In the dozen or so restaurants and bars where they had dined, his Italian suits, chiseled good looks and sophisticated repartee blended into the woodwork. But, here, overlooking Central Park, in his (in all but name, *his*) sprawling apartment Tory would see him in a different light. He served coffee and cognac in the living room.

"May I thmoke?" Tory asked.

"Be my guest," Larry said, rushing to place a Lalique candy dish in her hand. There were no ashtrays. Dolly didn't allow smoking in the apartment. Larry's pot smoking occurred behind closed doors with the window open.

Stretching out on the sofa, Tory kicked off her heels and curled her feet under her like a cat. A big, golden, satisfied cat.

"One thing I don't understand about you," she said, blowing out a long plume of smoke. "How is it possible you're still thingle?"

Larry weighed his reply carefully. So much hung in the balance.

"I'll be right back," he said

Tory sipped her cognac and leafed through *The New Yorker*, thinking Larry had excused himself to go to the bathroom. She was absorbed in a review of a Woody Allen film when a striking brunette in a black dress sat beside her and crossed her long, shapely legs.

"This is why I'm still single," Larry said.

46

Dirty dishes were in the sink the following morning when Ruth came in to make coffee. Her mother's finest china was caked with food. Larry hadn't bothered to rinse them and put them in the dish washer. Geneva's job was to take care of Dolly and do basic household chores. Not to be Larry's personal maid. Lately, Ruth tidied up after her brother. Not this time. She picked up the greasy broiler pan and stormed into Larry's room. It was 8 a.m.

"This isn't a hotel," she yelled, throwing the pan on his bed. Larry opened one mascaraed eye, then the other.

"What's your problem?" he asked hoarsely.

"My problem is that you are living here as if Mother can still take care of you. She *can't*. We all have to do our part, Larry. The least you can do is clean up after yourself. Wash your own dishes. Do your own laundry. Make your own bed. Geneva is giving us as much of her time as she can but she's can't do everything."

It was the most she had said to him in six months. She was shaking from the effort.

"Is that real?" Larry asked, staring at Ruth's left hand. She followed his eyes as if she had forgotten she was wearing a knockout diamond. *Oops. There it was.* She had meant to remove it.

"Where did you get it?" Larry said.

"In a Crackerjack box."

"You're engaged?" Larry asked, taking a closer look at the ring.

"We have an *understanding*."

"And what, pray tell, does that mean?"

"It means mind your own fucking business."

Witty's proposal had given Ruth something she didn't have before. Balls. Katya was right. A brilliant diamond, of substantial size, bestowed special powers on its wearer. The meek became assertive, the fearful became courageous and Ruth Sheraton, who had been on the receiving end of Larry's machinations, wasn't going to take it anymore.

Larry wasn't put off by Ruth's tirade. He was inspired. Last night had gone so well that he wasn't sure how to follow-up on it until he saw Ruth's ring. Yes, that would cinch it. A drop-dead diamond. Tory certainly deserved one. When he told her of his desire for gender reassignment surgery, she had nodded empathetically and asked him if he longed for a male partner.

"No. I'm not gay," he had explained. "I've never been attracted to men. I want to share my life with a woman who will accept me for who I am."

They had hugged for a long time and when Larry finally had the courage to look into Tory's eyes, he saw the acceptance he had always wanted. They kissed, tentatively at first, then deeply. Larry reveled in Tory's passionate response. And Tory yielded to the excitement of making love with a gorgeous woman.

47

"A diamond like that demands a celebration," Katya said. "An engagement party."

"At my age?" Ruth balked.

"Why not?"

Because I'm in love with someone else. Katya was bubbling with restaurants, menus and stationers. As much as Ruth dreaded the prospect, she knew that stopping Katya was as futile as trying to stop the Uptown Express after it left the station. Besides, it was just a party. Nothing set in stone. Just in fois gras at Per Chance, the most expensive restaurant in Manhattan. When Ruth protested the cost, Larry insisted on picking up the tab.

"You deserve it," he said. "You've done more than your fair share for Mother."

Ruth was caught off guard by this unexpected gesture of extravagance. Ever since Tory came into his life, Larry was less caustic, more empathetic. And generous. People can change. It was the basis of every 12-step program and the underlying myth of every Hollywood movie. But in Ruth's experience, the opposite was true. What you see is what you get. Still, she worried about the prospect of her louder-than-thou family running head on into Witty's country club clan.

"Don't worry," Katya said. "With the right seating plan, I could make peace in the Middle East."

The evening of the party, Ruth was so distracted by Witty's colorful siblings, she almost forgot about her own.

His brother Otto was a beer-bellied, golf cart salesman who bragged about the number of "sun spots" the doctor had removed from his head. Megan, Witty's older sister, wore a bright pink headband on her sun-streaked pageboy and had taken the train from Darien without ever leaving the bar car. She flagged down a waiter for a "dry, dry, dry martini" before they were seated. In the presence of his relatives, Witty seemed withdrawn and sheepish.

"Are you alright?" she asked.

"I'm fine. Fine," he murmured. "It's just that I don't see my family very often and when I do, well, it's as if I still should be sitting at the children's table."

"There's a cure for that," she said, placing her hand on Witty's thigh and giving it an amorous squeeze. The tension on his face dissolved into gratitude.

"What would I do without you?" he said.

Marry someone who isn't cheating on you.

Larry and Tory were the last to arrive. He in a trim dark grey suit, cobalt shirt and silver tie. She in a flowing navy Eileen Fisher ensemble. They looked so normal, Ruth was sure it was all smoke and mirrors.

"You see?" Katya whispered into Ruth's ear. "Everyone's getting along."

And they were. Aunt Miri attended to Dolly who kept asking, "What holiday is this?" Naomi sat quietly immersed in her crewelwork while her husband Howie chatted with Otto about his tax problems and Katya's husband offered Megan a complimentary consultation on her drooping eyelids. Tory and Megan quickly discovered their commonality. Both had gone to Briarcliffe and were "dear friends" of Sissy and Jib Newell of Newport. After the first round of Champagne toasts, Larry stood up and tapped his glass until all eyes were on him.

"On this happy occasion of Ruth and Witty's engagement, I would like to ask my dearest friend Tory Van Hooten to do me the great honor of being my wife," Larry said, then he dropped to one knee and held up a tiny blue box. Women shrieked. Men hooted and banged their fists on the table.

"Oh! Oh! My gawd!" Tory gasped, her eyes brimming, cheeks flushed, hands wriggling at the ends of her arms like freshly caught trout.

Ruth sat frozen while everyone took turns pumping Larry's hand, slapping him on the back and kissing Tory. She was too numb to notice that the diamond on Tory's hand belonged to her mother. An icy wave of déjà vu pulled Ruth back to her sixteenth birthday, swept her under, then dumped her roughly on the unforgiving shore of the present. Larry did what he had always done. He stole the show.

* * * *

Dinner had been exquisite. Caviar, lobster en croute. The works. Washed down with buckets of Tattinger's. But the only taste that lingered in Ruth's mouth was bile.

"I swear to God, my brother will tap dance on my grave just to draw attention to himself."

"Perhaps he was just caught up in the moment," said Witty.

"You don't know Larry," she said through gritted teeth.

They walked along Broadway arm in arm. This wasn't the conversation Ruth wanted to be having, but she couldn't stop herself.

"For my sixteenth birthday, my mother gave me a choice. A luncheon like all the other girls had or a special treat, a day of beauty at Elizabeth Arden. I took the day of beauty. For weeks, it was all I could think about. I would pass through that infamous red door, a frizzy-haired teenager, and emerge a femme fatale. But when the day finally arrived, my brother conveniently had one of his fainting spells. My mother rushed off to take Larry to a doctor and cancelled my appointment."

"Couldn't she have sent you off to Arden's in a cab?" Witty said.

"Not in the state she was in. Mom thought Larry was dying. Like it was a brain tumor or something. I fell for it too. So when the doctor said Larry was fine, Mom celebrated by taking him to see Cats. For the seventh time."

"Did you ever have your day of beauty?"

"A week later. But it wasn't the same. My sixteenth birthday had come and gone. Larry had ruined it. On purpose."

Witty put his arm around Ruth and drew her close. It was Saturday night. The sidewalks were filled with young couples on dates, Orthodox Jewish families with double-wide baby carriages and senior citizens walking off their solitary, coffee shop dinners.

"Do you think your brother is happy?" he asked.

"I don't know. You saw him. What do you think?"

"I think anyone who works so hard to get attention is crying out for love and acceptance."

"Love?" Ruth snorted. Larry's always been my mother's favorite."

"What about your father?"

Ruth gazed in the window of Harry's Shoes. Witty's even-keeled attempt at understanding, as if she were pleasure craft he was guiding through choppy waters, was driving her crazy. He never argued. Never exploded. Never told her she was fucking nuts. (As her friends did with regularity.) *He doesn't understand a word I'm saying. He never will. Until death do us part. DEATH!*

She had not told her friends in Los Angeles about her engagement out of fear it would bring bad luck, the *kina hera* that threatens to destroy all Jewish happiness foretold. Now, Ruth had another reason for holding off on the news. She was engaged, yes. But perhaps to the wrong man.

The debate inside her head was not civilized. It was a shouting match. Witty was the kind of man she had avoided all her life. Rich. Predictable. Fastidious in his dress and manners. A temperament so even one could balance Waterford crystal on it. His eyes never undressed other women. Or men. His devotion to Ruth was almost religious in its constancy. *Once he really knows me, he'll HATE me.*

Alex, on the other hand, was Ruth's type. Mercurial, marginally employed, mysterious. *What does he do when I'm not around?* He would talk for hours then suddenly go silent, looking at her through half-closed eyes. Did he miss his wife? Was he comparing Ruth unfavorably to a bronzed Italian heiress in a tiny white bikini on a yacht in the Adriatic? It wasn't that the voices championing Alex were more eloquent. It was that they were louder.

48

"Selma? This is Ruth Sheraton. You were at my father's shiva."

"Oh, yes, dear. How can I help?"

"I'd like to make an appointment."

"Certainly, is it urgent or something that can wait til next week?"

Ruth hesitated. Her life would still be a mess a week from now, but if she didn't see Selma soon, she'd lose her nerve. Ruth was like most sophisticated women of a certain age. She didn't *believe* in astrology. But in moments of angst and indecision, she was susceptible to the gravitational pull of the moon and stars.

"I don't want to wait that long."

"I can squeeze you in this afternoon at two-thirty if it's just facial hair. Anything down below, I'll need a larger block of time."

"I beg your pardon?"

"You're calling for electrolysis, right?"

"I must've dialed wrong. I'm looking for Selma Rifkin the astrologist."

"Why didn't you say so? That's my *other* business. Lucky for you, I have a cancellation. See you at two-thirty."

Selma Rifkin's multiplicity of careers puzzled Ruth but did not dissuade her. In Los Angeles, everyone was a hyphenate. People sold insurance, walked dogs *and* starred in pornographic films, depending on what day it was. Why not an astrologer who removed unwanted hair? Ruth stood in the foyer of a red brick apartment building on Minetta Street and pressed the buzzer marked S. Rivkin. Anyone who lived on such a charming street in the Village must have an inside track on the workings of the cosmos or, at least, Manhattan real estate.

Selma was a short, thin woman, considerably older than Ruth had remembered, with deep-set eyes in what had once been a pretty face. Selma collected her fee up front, stuffing the seventy-five dollars into the pocket of her pink cotton smock. It was a studio apartment with a Murphy bed hidden behind folding doors. Ruth had seen Murphy beds in old movies but had no idea they still existed. They sat at a small table on which Selma laid out a deck of cards.

"I thought you do astrology," Ruth said.

"You don't want cards?" Selma looked disappointed.

"Well, I don't know…"

"Tell you what. We'll do both. No extra charge. When's your birthday?"

"December 12, 1969."

"Sagittarius? You're a communicator. But you're sending out mixed messages lately."

Selma split the deck and shuffled.

"I want you to concentrate on a problem," she said laying cards on the table.

Just one?

"This is you," Selma said, tapping the three of clubs, "This is what surrounds you."

Selma pulled a pack of Marlboros out of her smock.

"You mind?"

Ruth shook her head.

"Some people do," Selma muttered. She paused to take a drag from her cigarette, then pointed at the ace of spades. "You had a relationship that ended traumatically. A divorce or death."

Who hasn't?

"There's a conflict involving money."

This was nonsense. Ruth was ready to get up and leave when Selma put one bony hand to her head, revealing the faint trace of numbers on her speckled forearm. Ruth did the math. If Selma was ninety, and she looked every bit of it, she had been eighteen in 1939.

"How did you know my father?" Ruth asked, thinking that Selma might be one of the Holocaust refugees her father's family had sponsored.

"Your father?"

"Sol Sheraton? You were at his *shiva*."

Selma shrugged.

"But you knew him, right?"

"I'll tell you the truth, dear. I read the obits and go to funerals because it's good for business. People who've suffered a loss are looking for answers. And they usually put out a nice spread."

"So you take advantage of their sorrow?" she said.

"I do no such thing." Selma was indignant. "I have a *gift*."

"Well, you haven't told me anything I don't already know."

Selma pinched the skin between her eyes.

"A good surgeon doesn't go in with a hacksaw. He makes the smallest cut possible, removes only what's diseased and leaves no scar. That's what I do. If I were to tell people everything I see the minute they sit down, they'd have a heart attack."

A black cat with round yellow eyes sprang into Selma's lap. She petted it absentmindedly with one hand while turning cards with the other, her cigarette ash dangling precariously.

"You've got a lot of conflict going on here," Selma said. "What kind of work do you do?"

"I'm a writer."

"This nine of diamonds indicates a new business deal. Big money. It may involve a move."

"I don't think so. I mean, I moved here from LA last fall and I have no plans to go back."

"Have it your way," Selma shrugged.

She tapped the table with an arthritic finger. "There's romance here...You've got the king of diamonds, a grey-haired guy with a lot of money and status. And you got this here jack of clubs. Younger, dark, more fun, right?"

Ruth nodded. Selma sighed and slapped down another card. The two of spades.

"Uh oh," she said.

"What? What?"

"The end of a relationship."

I'm going to get caught. Alex is going to find out about Witty or vice versa.

"The thing is, neither of these men are compatible with you, astrologically speaking," said Selma. "One is too fiery, the other is all air. You're water, mutable, you need someone with a lot of earth to ground you. A Taurus would be good."

Right. I'll post a personals ad on JDate. 42 SJF Sagittarian seeks Taurus mensch with earth moving equipment.

"You're surrounded by jealousy, but see here, the five of diamonds? That's a change for the better. Good things are coming your way. So think about starting a new project or having another child."

"I don't have children."

"You're young. It's not too late. Me? I prefer cats."

The black cat was now grooming himself, legs spread wide, tongue lapping madly.

"You're very close to your mother," Selma said. "She's a water sign like you, right?"

"Yes, she's a Pisces. Both my parents are. Or were. My father died in October."

"You miss him and you're worried about her. But you have to learn to let go."

"Let go?"

"How shall I say this?" Selma said. "Your father's spirit is in flux. The more you worry about your mother, the harder it is for him to pass on to the Other Side. He needs to know it's okay to go, that you can manage."

"But my mother can't manage on her own and I can't stop worrying about her."

"Worrying doesn't help. Have more confidence in yourself. You'll always have loving memories of your father, but you need to let him go and move on with your life."

The door bell rang.

"Oops," said Selma, gathering up the cards. "That's my next appointment. The hair I've removed from her legs, I could braid a rug."

Ruth stumbled outside, blinking into the slanting golden light of late afternoon. She walked aimlessly through the Village, her hands deep in her pockets. Selma hadn't answered her question. Witty or Alex? And her premonitions about a "big move" and a baby were off the charts. That's what astrologers say to everyone. Talking about travel and pregnancy probably results in a big tip. But the idea that her father was stranded, as if he had missed a connecting flight at JFK, was absurd. Although it was true that Ruth resented having to fill his shoes. *If Daddy were alive he would know what to do.* She stood in front of a vintage shop on Perry Street and gazed at the tortoise shell handbags, "I'm doing the best I can, Dad," she sighed.

"That's all I ask, Sweetheart."

Ruth saw her father's reflection in the shop window. Not the old, balding man he had become, but the younger, trimmer version she remembered from when she was in high school. She whipped around. No one was there.

49

"Are you sure this is what you want?"

"It's what I've *always* wanted," said Larry.

Tory snuggled closer under the covers and let her hand drift down between his legs. Ever since their first ecstatic union at the El Coronado, their frequent and noisy sexual encounters occurred exclusively at Tory's apartment.

"I'm tho fond of it, it doesn't seem fair," she said. "I mean, won't you mith it? I thertainly will."

He turned towards her and cupped her face in his hands.

"No, you won't. I promise." He kissed her deeply, long and hard, then grazed down, down, down until her breathing yielded to a calliope of pleasure.

Later, over coffee and cherry scones, Tory broached the subject again.

"But I don't understand," she said. "You have the best of both worlds now. Why thuch drastic, irreversible thurgery?"

"Because *this*," letting his robe fall open, "Isn't who I am."

"Thuppose you change your mind?"

"I won't. But if you do, it will kill me."

She looked across the kitchen table in disbelief. Men had never pursued Tory other than for mixed doubles. She had had her fair share of mercy fucks in her twenties and thirties, but hadn't had a reason to shave her legs in over a decade. Now here was a handsome, brilliant, sexy man asking her permission to chop off his penis.

"If I don't want you to do it, then what?" she asked.

Larry paled.

"Then I won't go through with it." His voice was no more than a whisper.

"Oh, come on, Larry. If having the thurgery is tho vital to your happiness, what difference does it make what I think? God knows, you'll probably find Mr. Right before I do."

"You don't get it. I'm *not* gay. I've never been attracted to men. I'm a woman trapped inside a man's body who loves women. And the woman I love most in all the world is you, my darling, voluptuous Tory."

He took her hand, led her back to bed and assured her, yet again, that she will always come first. There are people who cannot bear to live alone. Larry, for all his vanity, was one of them. In Amsterdam, he had a constantly rotating assortment of female companions, some were professionals who traded sexual favors for legal advice, others were artsy types who thought his houseboat was "cool." The surgery wouldn't cure his chronic loneliness but Tory would. She was perfect. Successful. Rich. *Understanding.* If other men found her lacking in feminine beauty, that was their loss. Larry was a tit man. Underneath Tory's man-tailored suits were 38 DD breasts with highly responsive nipples. She was soft and warm like an old-fashioned, down-filled sofa, so much more comfortable to sleep with than a bony woman. Plus, there was something rare and wondrous about her inexperience and gratitude. How many women said "thank you" after they climaxed?

Tory brought Larry into her law firm, giving him an office and an assistant. The income allowed him to begin the required year of hormone treatments and dressing as a woman prior to surgery, a subject which Tory communicated to her staff with the utmost sensitivity. Larry came to work in a blunt-cut brunette wig and professional female attire. A Hermes scarf, Longchamps bag, Elsa Peretti earrings. This had a ripple effect on the women at the firm who upgraded their wardrobes to match Larry's (Laura's) finery. Before long, they were coming to him for advice. Do these shoes go with this dress? Is this lipstick too dark? Where did you get that necklace?

Tory, too, started dressing with more care and watching her diet, ordering salad instead of French fries, sorbet rather than ice cream. She dropped two sizes.

"Have you lost weight?" Larry asked over brunch at Le Pain Quotidien.

"A little," Tory said, thrilled he had finally noticed. Her goal was to drop another twenty pounds before inviting him to her beach house for moonlight skinny dipping.

"Well, don't lose any more."

"Why not?"

"Because I love you the way you are."

Tory blushed and ordered the chocolate croissant she had been denying herself for months.

50

"Where are we going?" Dolly asked.

"To the park," Ruth said.

Dolly's gait was unsteady. Ziskin had first prescribed a cane, then a walker. Both stood untouched in the hall closet. Dolly preferred hanging onto the walls and furniture or, in this case, clinging heavily onto Ruth's arm.

"So many cars," Dolly said.

There were no more or less cars on Central Park West than before. But Dolly, who hadn't been out of the apartment all winter had no memory of the street on which she had lived for half a century.

"Where are we going?" she repeated.

"The park."

"So many cars."

Ruth had dressed her mother in beige slacks, a matching sweater and a light windbreaker. It was more than what most people were wearing that warm spring day, but Ruth knew that the elderly had their own thermostat. The playground was a short walk from the park's entrance. Ruth steered her mother to an empty bench.

"I know this place," Dolly said.

"Of course, you do. You used to take us here all the time. Remember when I fell from the swing?"

Dolly looked befuddled. Ruth had broken the first commandment of caring for a loved one with dementia. Do not ask if they remember. Stick to the present, the only time in which they exist. But she could still employ the second commandment. Redirect.

"Look at that little girl," Ruth said, pointing at a child coming down the slide. "Isn't she adorable?"

Dolly brightened.

"I have three little girls," she said.

"No. You have two daughters."

"Don't tell me. I know how many daughters I have," Dolly insisted.

Oh fuck. What's wrong with me today? This was another thing she had read. Don't correct her mistakes. Remain positive.

"Do you have children?" Dolly asked Ruth.

"No, no I don't."

"That's okay," she said, patting Ruth's arm. "Someday you will."

If asked, Dolly would've stated that Ruth was in her twenties with her whole life ahead of her and that she, herself, was in her forties. Still in her prime with a husband and a carefree future. Ruth envied her mother's ability to push the reverse button of life and revisit happier times. Lately, Ruth felt precariously stuck in Fast Forward. The dissolution of her marriage, her father's death, Dolly's illness, her engagement to a man for whom she only felt gratitude and her growing realization that the careening lust she felt for Alex had taken a dangerous curve into Love. If only she could make it all slow down. She closed her eyes and breathed in the magnolia scented air.

"Is that your Mommy?" said a high-pitched voice.

It was Bennie, Margot's daughter, in denim overalls and a Curious George t-shirt. Her orange hair was now cut short like a boy's. Dolly was enchanted. She had always loved children but with the onset of dementia she became absolutely gaga over them.

"Yes, honey. This is my mommy," Ruth said. "Is your mommy here today?"

Bennie nodded and returned moments later with Margot. Ruth introduced Dolly who smiled warmly and made appropriate remarks, commenting on Bennie's pretty blue eyes and Margot's magenta blouse. The third time Dolly commented on her blouse Margot looked at Ruth questioningly, then told Bennie to play in the sandbox. It's not contagious, Ruth wanted to scream. But maybe it was. Since Dolly's lights had dimmed, Ruth felt that she too was swimming in quicksand, losing her keys, leaving her credit card behind in the ATM, firing up her laptop then forgetting what she wanted to do. *Redirect!* Ruth focused on a dark, curly-haired boy hanging by his knees from the jungle gym. He looked like Paulo, Alex's boy. She had only met him once or twice. It was only when a woman shouted "Paulo, be careful!" that Ruth knew for sure. The woman was in her late twenties. She had a long, corn silk pony tail that swung as she scooped Paulo up in her arms. Alex had never mentioned a nanny but she fit the description. Young, trim, wearing one of those fake retro t-shirts, skinny jeans and red Converse high tops.

"Do you know her?" Ruth asked Margot.

"I've seen her but we never talked."

"The boy's father is…is a friend. I'd like to say hello. Could you sit with my mother? I'll be right back."

Ruth jumped up before Margot could protest. As she got closer to the nanny, Ruth noted the girl's toned arms, flat stomach and creamy complexion. A college student or an aspiring model. She had the height. Ruth, at five-feet-eight considered herself tall. But the nanny towered over her.

"Hi Paolo," Ruth said.

The boy looked at Ruth and smiled uncertainly, then went back to his toy truck.

"I'm Ruth Sheraton," Ruth said, sticking out her hand. "I'm a friend of Paolo's father."

"Oh, gosh. You're the writer?" the nanny gushed. "I'm Kelly."

Ruth grinned. Alex had talked about her to the nanny. Good sign.

"Alex is so excited about working with you," Kelly said.

Working? Is that what he calls it? Well, she's just the nanny.

"He's been wanting to make the leap from short stories to screenplays for so long and you've been so supportive," Kelly said. "I can't tell you how much it means to us."

Us?

Kelly chattered on, playing with her pony tail. Something glinted on her left hand. It was a modest diamond, barely half a carat. Ruth knew her jealousy was irrational, insane, obscene. And yet she would've pulled off her flawless diamond and traded it on the spot. If Alex came with it.

Margot shouted Ruth's name from the other side of the playground.

"Gotta go," Ruth said.

"I'll tell Alex I saw you," Kelly said.

"Yes. You do that."

Ruth returned to the bench to find her mother greatly agitated.

"My watch!" Dolly cried, extending her bare wrist. "Somebody stole my watch."

Sure enough, the slender gold band was missing. Ruth searched her mother's pockets, coming up with a crumpled dollar, a KitKat and a wad of Kleenex. Dolly had probably left the watch on the sink. Or in the freezer. Ruth thanked Margo for watching Dolly and guided her mother out of the park, a slow and humbling task, every crack in the sidewalk a potential broken hip or dislocated shoulder. It suddenly occurred to Ruth why Kelly looked familiar. The flaxen-hair, lithe body, amber eyes. She was the love interest Alex described in his screenplay. *She is his future. I'm not.* Ruth doubled over and puked in the hedges.

51

"You told her I was helping you with your *writing*?" Ruth asked.

"I was trying to be discreet. My mother and Paolo have seen you come to the apartment. What did you want me to say? This is Ruth, we have hot, crazy sex?"

Ruth stared at the knife Alex was using to slice avocados. She wondered if it was sharp enough to separate his head from his body.

"That's all we're about? Sex?" she said.

Alex put down the knife and wiped his eyes with his shirt sleeve. His tears weren't for her, they were from the red onions he sliced to gossamer thinness.

"That first night. Remember what you said?" he asked, "You said, I can follow a strong lead. That's all I've been doing, Ruth. Following your lead. You come here twice a week, we eat, we talk, we make love."

He poured olive oil and balsamic vinegar over the avocados and onions. "I have no idea who you see when you're not with me," he said. "But I'm not naïve. I know I am not the only man in your life."

There was no anger in his voice, only disappointment. Ruth stared at the table set with cobalt Fiesta Ware on a tangerine cloth.

"Why do you say that?" she asked. "Do I talk in my sleep?"

Alex closed his tragic, deep-set eyes and massaged his temples.

"Ruth, it isn't what you've said. It's what you never *asked*." He wiped his hands on a dish towel. "You never asked what I do when we're not together."

"If I had...?"

Alex shrugged.

"I would've lied." He said. "The same as you would've lied to me. Because both of us want this fantasy to be real even though it's impossible."

"But you're *engaged*....how could you...?"

"There is more than one kind of love, Ruth." Alex said, gazing at her in that way he had, through thickly lashed, sleepy brown eyes. "I thought what we had was rare and beautiful. It doesn't have to end like this." His voice was just above a whisper.

Oh, my god, she thought, he thinks I'm here for a goodbye fuck. And, sure enough, Alex did what he had done so many times before. He put a Piazzolla tango on the M3 player. Wordlessly, he held out his hand to lead her to his bed. It would've been so easy. The weight of his body on hers once more, the taste of his skin, that wild high of endorphins. No one would ever know. Ruth grabbed her jacket and raced out the door.

* * * *

"What's wrong with me, Gabby? Why can't I have a normal life?"

"Because we don't *do* normal, Pumpkin. We're showbiz. We do edgy, dangerous, whacky. Anything but normal. That's for people in Ohio."

206

"But I was so happy with Alex," she cried.

"Let me ask you something," Gabby said. "Where did Alex the Magnificent take you?"

Ruth drew a blank.

"*Take* me?" she said.

"Yeh. You know, open his wallet and show you a good time."

Ruth thought.

"Well, he once took me to dinner at a little Italian place and dancing downtown."

"*Once?*" Gabby's painted brows shot up.

Ruth had never thought about it before. After than first date, he hadn't taken her anywhere but so what?

"All these months you've been staring at this guy's bedroom ceiling and he didn't spend one fucking dime?" Gabby howled.

"That's not true. He cooked for me."

Gabby didn't understand. Ruth had been at her happiest watching Alex cook *arroz con frioles negros* in his boxers. Their relationship was too passionate, too raw to parade all over town.

"Did he meet your friends? Did you meet his?" Gabby pummeled.

Ruth put her hand to her mouth. The picture Gabby was painting was distorted but if Ruth squinted, it came into focus. He *was* her Fuck Monkey!

"Poor Baby," Gabby said. "All you have now is a millionaire who wants to wrap you in ermine and pearls. Do I hear violins?"

"But I don't *love* him," Ruth wailed.

"Just promise you won't let your personal *drek* interfere with writing for me," Gabby said, grabbing Ruth's cheeks with both hands and pinching hard.

"I promise."

"Oh, and one more thing. That ring? Don't even *think* of giving it back."

52

Naomi's counseling job at Megillah University was something she could do in her sleep, as many a bewildered student discovered when she began to snore. Her purpose, as defined by the dean of students, was to make sure that students did not commit suicide, murder or rape on her watch and, if they did, to wash the blood off the University's hands as quickly as possible. Depression, drug problems, failing grades, roommates from Hell and abortions, the flotsam and jetsam of college life, were to be handled discreetly. The Counseling Office was not there to provide psychological services in the traditional sense, but, like a traffic cop, to direct students to the nearest exit ramp. Since 99% of the students were Orthodox Jews, this was achieved by a call to a rabbi whom Naomi had on speed-dial.

On the day in question, Naomi was nodding off while a sophomore whined on and on about a boy who wouldn't leave her alone. Helping twenty-year-old virgins fend off horny guys was one of the more entertaining aspects of her work, but today Naomi couldn't focus. All she could think about was Shoshanna. She wasn't answering emails or calls, and more disturbingly, hadn't asked for money in weeks.

The student in the chair was full to bursting in the bra department and had a sweet, if slightly dopey, face. Such a girl would marry early, hatch out a child a year until she went through menopause and always live walking distance from her mother. She doesn't have problems, Naomi thought. I, *I* have problems.

"Tell me," Naomi said, interrupting the girl's monologue. "Would you ever ignore an email or phone message from your mother?"

"Uh, no."

"Ah hah! Just what I thought" Naomi pounced forward, wagging her finger. "And would you shack up with a man you hardly knew just because he was rich and could give you whatever your heart desired?"

The girl squirmed in her chair, repulsed by the thought.

"No," she said, "I want a husband who shares my values, who will devote himself to a lifetime of studying the Talmud," she said.

"See? See? You have good values. You don't need me or anyone else to tell you how to deal with this sexed up boy. But you may want to get yourself a better fitting bra and wear less revealing sweaters."

As soon as the shaken girl hoisted her backpack, Naomi flipped open her phone.

"Dr. Ramussen? It's Naomi Karp. I have an urgent problem," she said.

"Have you tried chanting?" Ramussen held up one finger to the naked young man lying next to him, signaling he would be but a moment.

"Yes, yes but it's not working. It's my daughter. I've lost her," Naomi's voice crept into a higher register, somewhere between fingernails drawn across a blackboard and a dog whistle.

"You're hyperventilating. You need to breathe, my dear. Deep breaths. Come, come. Breathe with me," Ramussen said as the boy slid ever so slowly down his body, using his tongue like a washcloth.

Naomi and Ramussen breathed deeply together, Naomi inhaling and exhaling on her end of the line. "AHHHHHHHHHHHHH!" the guru moaned as the boy slurped his inner thighs. "That was a cleansing breath. Are you feeling better?" he asked Naomi.

"Yes, a bit. But I need to see you. I can't do this on my own."

"Well, I'm interviewing a, uh, personal assistant at the moment, but I could see you at six," said Ramussen. "Remember, Naomi. You are gifted. You must release, release, release…"

His voice trailed off, then Naomi thought she heard laughter. Only a holy man like Dr. Ramussen could do that, absorb her pain and turn it into joy. She looked at her appointment book and chewed her lip. Three students, all with problems that paled in comparison to her own, would troop through her office before she could leave. To compensate for this gross injustice, Naomi leafed through *Modern Knitting Magazine* and ate a Peanut Chew while the students addressed their grievances to her nodding head.

* * * *

Dr. Ramussen's office was located above Roscoe's Tropical Fish. There was no name on the buzzer but an index card with "The Way," written in ornate calligraphy, was taped to a peeling door on the second floor. A Mexican kid in tight jeans descended the stairs as Naomi climbed up. She jangled Tibetan bells hanging from the door knob. A moment later, Ramussen opened the door wearing a flowing white linen caftan and a beatific smile. Radiating well-being, he invited Naomi to sit in the Meditation Room.

Naomi lowered herself onto a squishy cushion and gazed into the flame of the thick, round three-foot candle on the altar. Sometimes a phallus is just a phallus. Incense burned, not quite covering up the aroma of curried eggplant.

"Let's start by chanting," he said, sitting in the lotus position directly in front of her, their knees almost touching.

"I deeply and completely accept myself...." they said in unison, over and over until it became a steady drone.

Opening her eyes, Naomi was struck, yet again, by Dr. Ramussen's beauty. He was the most attractive man she had ever known. His skin was copper and his features were an exotic stew of Indian, Jamaican and African. And that voice! So caressing and melodious. She assumed he had a doctorate in philosophy or religion from a university in far-off Cairo, Mumbai or Helsinki when, in fact, Ramussen's academic career had ended when he walked out of Walt Whitman Middle School in Brooklyn to score some weed and never returned.

"Let me look into your soul," he said, grasping her hands.

Naomi's heart lurched. She had not been touched by a man other than her gynecologist in over a year. She averted her eyes, ashamed of what she was feeling.

"Look at me," he urged.

Naomi looked. Her breathing quickened. Her pulse raced. Her womb hummed. She felt tingling in places she had thought were closed for repair. Ramussen stepped out of his caftan and helped Naomi out of her clothes. What happened in the next forty-five minutes was something Naomi would never be able to explain. She only knew that when she walked back out on 29th Street, her daughter was the least of her problems.

53

"For heaven's sake. Can't a person have some privacy?" Dolly was sitting on the toilet. She had shut the door but Sol followed her into the bathroom anyway. Lately, he had been doing that. Never giving her a moment's peace.

"What's that freeloader doing here again?" Sol asked, perching on the edge of the tub. "Doesn't he have a home?"

"Mr. Greenbaum is lonely. I'm lonely. Since when is it a crime for two lonely people to have a piece of cake and a cup of tea?"

"Because that's how it starts." Sol said, "The next thing you know, he'll be too tired to take the elevator back to his place. He'll be sleeping in *my* bed."

"How dare you. In all the years we were married… I never *looked* at another man but you, you…"

"Enough already," Sol said. "I know my sins, all one hundred and sixty-two of them. They keep track up there. It's worse than the IRS. No loopholes. No extensions. But here's the thing, Dolly. I'm lonely too."

Sol Sheraton, who'd peeked under every skirt from Washington Square to the Bronx, lonely? Impossible.

"What are you talking about?" Dolly said.

"I'm not a fool, Dolly. Foolish? Yes. A fool? No. I always knew I couldn't live without you. And now I realize, I can't die without you either."

His voice shook. A single tear made its way from his eye, down his prodigious nose and dangled from its tip.

"I don't understand," said Dolly, handing him a tissue. "What do you want from me?"

"Come. Come with me."

Dolly was still on the toilet. She hadn't done what she came there to do. She couldn't. Not with Sol standing over her.

"Give me a minute. Alone," she said.

Sol left. Dolly sat there thinking. How could she take off with Sol when Bernie Greenbaum was waiting for her in the next room? That would be rude. This was all so upsetting. If she went with Sol, what should she pack? Just casual or something dressy? Dolly flushed the toilet and washed her hands. When she stepped into her bedroom, Sol was standing there with his coat on, looking at his watch.

"*Nu?*" he said.

"Just let me grab a few things." Dolly opened her closet. Where had all these clothes comes from?

"We're not going to Vegas," Sol bellowed. "You're fine in what you're wearing. Maybe take a sweater. It's drafty there."

All married couples have certain arguments that repeat like garlic. For the Sheratons, it was packing. Sol never understood why it took Dolly three weeks and a new set of luggage to prepare for a weekend in the Catskills. To take or not to take. Every bra and slip became a Supreme Court decision.

Ruth, who had been chatting with Mr. Greenbaum while Dolly was indisposed, found her mother carefully folding a blouse into a suitcase.

"What are you doing?" Ruth asked.

"Oh, hello, dear," Dolly responded with a warm smile. "I'm going away with your father."

This was a new one. Sometimes it was best to play along.

"Where exactly are you and Daddy going?" asked Ruth.

A cloud of confusion settled over Dolly's face.

"I don't know," she said.

"Well, how about a cup of tea and some cake for the road?"

It wouldn't hurt to have a nosh. Why travel on an empty stomach? Dolly looked around for Sol. He was gone. Just like him. Always in a rush then nowhere to be found. She followed the young woman, who might or might not be her daughter, hard to tell with so many people coming and going.

54

Hassan Maloof, the international art dealer responsible for Witty's rise and fall, lived on the top two floors of one of the new glass towers that shimmered over the East Hudson. Ceilings were tented in pale blue silk. The only furnishings were burgundy velvet lounges lining the walls, leaving a vast space for his two hundred guests to drink Dom Perignon and admire his most recent acquisition. Titian's *Salome.*

"I thought that painting was in a museum in Rome," Ruth said.

"It is," Witty replied. "Hassan believes Titian painted more than one version. It's causing quite a stir. Sometimes I think that he enjoys the controversy more than the art itself."

"But it could be a forgery, right?" Ruth said under her breath. She was in no mood to be sipping Champagne and admiring a mogul's art collection. Ever since confronting Alex, it was all she could do just to get out of bed.

"Ah, there you are, my friend," said a short, bald man with a paintbrush black mustache. He kissed Witty on both cheeks then turned to Ruth, taking her hand and brushing it with his furry lips. "And who is this beautiful desert flower?"

"Hassan, this is Ruth Sheraton. Ruth is a television writer."

Hassan's eyes narrowed

"Ruth? That is a Hebrew name, is it not?"

"Yes," she said.

"I am very fond of your people," Hassan said.

Ruth was not sure where this was going.

"Tell me, Ruth," Hassan smiled mischievously. "Why do they call Israel the Jhooish State? There are more Jhoos in New York than in Tel Aviv."

Hassan laughed raucously, then faded into the crowd.

"That was awkward," said Ruth, grabbing another champagne flute off a passing tray.

"Oh, Hassan was just pulling your leg. He doesn't give a damn for politics or religion. That's why he keeps an apartment here where the modesty police won't tell his girlfriends to cover up."

"Girlfriends? I thought you said he has four wives? Are any of them here?"

"God no, they're all locked away in his palaces in Saudi Arabia. Hassan is a party animal. Notice all the tall, young, models?"

They entered a dining room flanked by gold urns large enough to accommodate Nubian slaves. There were no tables and chairs, just ornate cushions around the perimeter of the room.

"We're sitting on the floor?" Ruth asked.

"When in Rome or Medina…" said Witty, squatting on a cushion.

Once everyone was settled, the lights dimmed.

"What's going on?" Ruth whispered.

"One never knows with Hassan."

A gong sounded and young men in flowing white jalabas with tasseled red fezzes on their heads trooped into the room in groups of four, each group carrying a bier on their shoulders. Ceremoniously, the biers were lowered to the floor.

218

"My God. What *is* that?" Ruth asked Witty.

"Sushi. Thousands of dollars of sushi. Possibly millions. Incredible, isn't it? Hassan flies in top chefs from Japan."

"But, but, there's a woman under all that fish."

Lying immobile on a bed of dewy watercress, her genitals a mound of glistening fish eggs, her nipples blossoming ginger rosettes was a naked young woman. As the shock wore off and guests began reaching for raw tuna with their chopsticks, Ruth attempted to help herself to a California roll on the woman's thigh.

"Isn't this perverse?" Ruth whispered to Witty. "He comes from a country where women can't leave the house without wearing a shroud and he serves up naked girls as if they were chopped liver."

Witty nodded, his mouth stuffed with yellow tail. Ruth continued to nibble around the edges of propriety. Women as dinnerware? This was sexism at its worst. Why wasn't anyone protesting and storming out? This was the Upper East Side, not Riyadh.

"I can't do this," she hissed.

"Come on, Ruth. Be a sport," Witty said. "If you don't want to eat now, we can go out for Chinese later."

Ruth sulked in silence but she couldn't take her eyes off the face of the young woman, staring blindly at the ceiling. Was she drugged? She looked familiar somehow. Those pouty lips. That nose. The mole on her neck. Ruth edged closer, leaning over the immobile, edible girl, staring directly into her unblinking eyes.

"Shoshanna?"

The human fish platter sprang up, SHRIEKED, and ran out of the room, clutching her bare breasts and leaving a trail of sushi in her wake.

55

"I'm sorry you lost your job," Ruth said to her niece the following afternoon. "But why would you want to be a fish platter? It's so…so….degrading and unsanitary."

"It's not degrading. It's performance art," Shoshanna said. "And it's not unsanitary. They made me cover my pussy with Saran Wrap."

"Sweetheart, people were *eating* off of you."

Shoshanna sat on the sofa, clutching a throw pillow to her chest, kicking her legs like a two-year-old.

"You going to tell my mother?" she said, squinting her eyes into half-moons.

Trick question. Saying yes would put an end to Shoshanna's visits which Dolly relished and Ruth depended upon. Saying no would give the green light to God knows what.

"You're over eighteen," Ruth said carefully. "You don't need your parents' permission or mine to take a job. But the choices you make now are important. They will set the pattern for your entire life."

It was bullshit. Ruth knew it. If the things she did when she was nineteen had predicted her future, she'd be working in a bordello. No. God protects those at the height of their fertility by making them invulnerable to their irresponsible, brain-dead, dumb-ass behaviors. Unprotected sex. Fast cars. Tequila shooters. Glue sniffing. Most teenagers pass through these tiger cages unscathed.

"I care about you," Ruth said. The words tasted lemony in her mouth. Sour and sweet.

"I knooooooooow," Shoshanna said, twirling her hair which now contained a streak of cobalt.

"There must be ways to make money without taking off your clothes," Ruth said.

Her niece's eyes glazed over. She was at the age in which an adult's voice, if it droned on too long, was sleep-inducing.

"I guess." Shoshanna stood, stretched into a yoga pose. Flying Warrior. A gold band twinkled on her wrist.

"Is that Grandma's watch?" Ruth asked.

"This old thing? Yeh," Shoshanna said, not breaking her pose. "I didn't want it. Grandma insisted."

Ruth was tempted to ask her to give the watch back but what purpose would it serve? Dolly would forget in two seconds and give the watch to Shoshanna all over again."Hey, you can go now," Shoshanna said, bending over into Downward Dog. "I'll watch Grandma."

For a big girl, she was surprisingly agile.

* * * *

"She takes after you," Katya said. "Remember Spring Break in Cancun? You hooked up with a guy you met on the beach and didn't come back to our hotel for a week. As I recall, he didn't speak a word of English and the only Spanish you knew was the menu at Taco Bell."

"That was different. I got naked with one boy. Not a room full of strangers."

They were lying on adjacent massage tables at H²O, a new spa on West 57th. Katya's treat. They had been scrubbed with Kosher salt and sesame oil, wrapped in seaweed and were resting with herbal pillows over their eyes. Electronic music that sounded like a fetal heartbeat wafted thru the darkened room.

"What about when you danced naked at the Pink Pussycat?" Katya said.

"I auditioned. I didn't work there," she snapped back. "You're the one who disrobed in public for over a year."

Ah, yes. Katya had appeared in an all-nude, musical version of King Lear that was so far off-Broadway, you had to turn left at Newark. That was the trouble with college friendships that stretched like discolored girdles to accommodate the passing decades. Each had become the repository of the other's most shameful memories. By reminding Ruth of her brief and humiliating stint as a topless "dancer" in a Village bar, Katya had gone too far.

"If I still had that body, I'd do it all over again," Katya laughed nervously. The thing is, Katya did have that body due to the surgical talents of her husband.

"Really? Wesley wouldn't mind?"

Silence.

"He couldn't care less," Katya said finally. "Do you have any idea how many tits he sees in a week?"

No argument there.

"You're right," Ruth sighed, "I guess Shoshanna does takes after me. Such a wild child. She'll never settle down and make a sensible marriage like you."

Sensible marriages were boring. And yet, wasn't that where Ruth was heading with Witty?

"What's wrong?" Katya asked. "Are you crying?"

"No. Must've gotten salt in my eye."

56

"There must be a mistake," Ruth explained to the person who called from Chase Bank. "My mother doesn't use credit cards anymore. We canceled them."

"According to our records, there was a charge on her Chase VISA last week for one thousand, three hundred dollars," Amber said. "I'm just calling to confirm."

Ruth rushed to the nearest Chase branch on Broadway.

"Tom Mathers," said a bank manager. "What can I do for you today?"

Mathers was a thick-necked man with ramrod posture, ice blue eyes, a military buzz cut and a *semper fidelis* pin in his lapel.

"I believe my mother is the victim of identity theft," Ruth said.

Mather's grin flattened into a somber, straight line.

"We cancelled all of her credit cards months ago. Mom has memory loss." Ruth explained, "But I got a call from the bank this morning. Someone's run up over a thousand dollars on a Chase credit card in her name, Dolly Sheraton."

"Is your name on her account as well?" he asked.

"Yes. Ruth Sheraton but I really haven't been involved. I'm not a numbers person. My brother Larry manages my mother's expenses."

Mathers tapped his keyboard, then spun the computer screen around so Ruth could see it.

"There are two ATM cards issued to the account," he said.

"That's impossible. My mother can't use an ATM anymore."

"One card was issued to Lawrence Sheraton and the other to Naomi Karp in late October," Mather said. "Both have been making weekly cash withdrawals of two to three hundred dollars."

"Jesus Christ." Ruth said.

Mathers shot her a look. She had taken his Lord's name in vain.

"The call you received this morning was just a courtesy call," he said. "We do that whenever there's a charge of over one thousand dollars with a payee that hasn't appeared on the account before. In this case, it was Per Chance."

"My engagement party," she said.

"So you recognize the charge?" he said.

"Yes. But. But…," Ruth stammered. "My brother told me *he* was paying for it."

"Well, he did," Mathers said. "Using the credit card linked to your mother's account. Technically, this isn't identity theft. It's a family matter."

Ruth stared at the monitor. All this time she had wondered how Larry could afford designer duds and extravagant bottle clubs. Now she knew. He was plundering her mother's estate. With Naomi cheering him on. *I'll kill him.*

"What can I do to stop this hemorrhage?" Ruth demanded.

"As I said. This is a family matter," he said.

"You don't understand," she cried. "We share power of attorney. We're supposed to be *protecting* her funds, not using them for our own purposes. What they're doing is illegal."

Mathers pushed a box of Kleenex in Ruth's direction and leaned towards.

"Unfortunately, this sort of, uh, misunderstanding happens more often than you'd think when an elderly family member becomes incapable of managing their own finances," he said. "However, since your name's on the account, there are things you can do…"

* * * *

Naomi finished reading an excerpt from her newest book *Past Imperfect: Embracing Your Failures* to a crowd of clinically depressed fans at the 92nd Street Y, then made her way to the lobby to sign books. A sign at her desk stated, "Out of consideration for those waiting in line, there will be no hand shaking or long conversations." Naomi wore white cotton gloves just in case.

"My parents discouraged me from being a dancer," said an obese matron in flesh-colored yoga pants..

Naomi nodded empathetically.

"I was the unhappiest corporate attorney in Manhattan," said a man in paint-splattered denim overalls. "After reading your first book, I quit my job, left my wife, moved into a barn in Jersey and started painting."

"I'm so happy for you," Naomi said.

"LIAR! CHEAT! THIEF!" hissed a woman.

Naomi looked up. It was Ruth.

"I know what you did. It's *embezzlement*," Ruth said.

The crowd stirred. People backed away.

"Please," Naomi said.. "Not *here.* There are people waiting.

"LET THEM WAIT," Ruth shouted. "I'm sure they all want to know how you *stole* from your frail, elderly mother."

"I did no such thing," Naomi said.

"What about those cash withdrawals you made every week?"

"I took her to lunch."

"Where? Alain Ducasse?"

A security guard grabbed Ruth's arm.

"Ma'am? I need you to step away from the line," he said.

"Get your fucking hands off me," Ruth yelled.

A second rent-a-cop appeared, grabbed Ruth's other arm and dragged her out of the auditorium, depositing her on the sidewalk.

* * * *

That night, Ruth and her mother sat in the den watching an episode of *In Treatment.* Dolly repeatedly remarked that Gabriel Byrne was "good enough to eat." Proof that dementia does not destroy one's vision. Larry came bounding into the room wearing a chartreuse cocktail dress.

"How dare you go sneaking around behind my back," he said.

"Me? You and Naomi were the ones who were sneaking around," said Ruth. "You were withdrawing Mother's money every week."

"Children, please," said Dolly. "I can't hear my program."

Larry and Ruth moved to the living room.

"I was mortified," he said, his left foot tapping. "Do you have any idea how it looked to Tory when my credit card was rejected at Jean-George? I called the bank they said you *closed* the account. Are you fucking nuts? YOU CAN'T DO THAT!"

"Oh, but I *can* and I did," Ruth purred.

"If you don't put my name and Naomi's back on mother's account immediately, I'm suing you," Larry said.

"For what? Protecting Mother?"

"Pul-lease. Who's going to protect her from you? You came here for one reason – free rent. You're a vulture, waiting to swoop down and pick her bones dry. If you think you're ever getting your hands on this apartment."

Larry stood so close, she felt his spittle on her face

"I don't want the apartment," she said. "I just want mother to live here as long as possible."

"Don't give me that crap," he yelled. "I know what you did to Naomi. You slandered her in public. She's taking out a restraining order against you and so am I."

"How you going to do that, Larry? I live here."

"Not for long," he said.

57

Dolly looked around for a clue, something to tell her where she was. A hotel room maybe? There was photo of a bride in a silver frame whom she recognized as herself. But who was that old woman in the mirror?

"May I have this dance?"

Dolly was relieved to see Sol. If he was here, she wasn't lost. He held out his hand and led her onto the dance floor. The band was playing *Fools Rush In*. Oh, what a wonderful dancer he was. So light on his feet. They glided, he pressed his cheek against hers. He dipped her low and pulled her high. At times, her feet didn't touch the floor. Sol sang along with the music. *When we met I felt my life begin…so open up your heart and let this fool rush in.*

"Oh, Baby. I've missed you so much," he said.

He swept her up off the floor. Around and around they twirled.

"Please, Sol, I'm getting dizzy," Dolly cried.

He wouldn't stop.

Geneva and Ruth came running. Dolly was on the floor, moaning like a wounded animal, her leg at an unnatural angle. EMTs arrived and took her on a gurney to the ER of Columbia Presbyterian where a young Pakistani resident examined her.

"She'll be alright?" Ruth said.

"I gave her something for pain but she needs surgery," the baby-faced doctor said. "We can admit her as soon as you sign the consent form."

Ruth started to sign then stopped.

"What kind of surgery?"

"Her femur is broken just below the hip. We'll have to insert a metal rod. She'll need rehab…"

"Rehab? My mother has dementia. Will she be able to walk again?"

"That's unlikely," said Baby Doc, bouncing on his feet.

"What about pain?"

Ruth looked at her mother who was resting quietly with the trace of a Demerol smile.

"We'll try to keep her comfortable but there'll be a long recovery process for a woman her age," he said.

"I need to think about this." Ruth said.

The resident spun on his heels and disappeared behind a white curtain.

"What's the matter, Ruth? You look so sad."

Ruth was startled. Her mother was speaking.

"Mom? Are you okay?"

"I've been better," Dolly said, smiling sheepishly

"They want you to have surgery. Is that what you want?"

Dolly made a face.

"Surgery? *Feh.*"

But what was the alternative? Ruth conferred with Geneva in the reception area.

"Your mama wouldn't like being confined to a wheelchair," said Geneva. "She's too proud. There has to be something else. What does Dr. Ziskin say?"

Ziskin! In her panic Ruth had forgotten about him. Cell phones weren't allowed in the ER. She stepped outside and called. When she came back, her face was ashen.

"What did he say?" Geneva asked.

Ruth spoke in gulps.

"He said we shouldn't put her through it. Dementia patients have a fifty-fifty chance of dying during surgery…and with her osteoporosis…."

"So what do we do?" asked Geneva.

Ruth's eyes welled up with tears. She could hardly get out the words.

"Hospice. He said…he said…the compassionate choice is to…to let her go."

"Let her go?" Geneva wailed. "Go where?"

"He said the only thing we can do is control her pain with morphine. She'll be gone within two weeks."

Ruth and Geneva clung to one another while, all around, people examined their fingernails. Death is the ER visitor nobody wants to acknowledge.

58

"Is it alright if I remove the crucifix?" Ruth asked.

"Whatever makes you comfortable," said the nurse adjusting Dolly's IV.

Dr. Ziskin had recommended Saint Bernadette's, a Catholic hospice on the Upper East Side. He assured them it was the Four Seasons of hospices. Ruth replaced the Madonna and cross with family photos. She filled vases with peach roses and baby's breath. It was more for her own comfort than her mother's, whose eyes had closed the day she arrived. Dolly was hooked up to a morphine drip with the official goal of controlling her pain and the unspoken knowledge that she would never wake up again.

The decision hadn't been Ruth's alone. Naomi came to the ER before Dolly was transferred to hospice in one of her knitwear creations, looking like nothing less than a macramé project gone wrong. Larry arrived soon after in a sedate taupe Anne Klein suit, silk blouse and stacked heel Ferragamo Oxfords. By then, Dolly was in a drug-induced sleep, her mouth slightly open. No one argued with the prognosis. Zisken had spoken. Dolly would be fast-tracked to that great kosher resort in the sky.

Ruth thought she read relief on her brother's and sister's faces. Relief and eagerness. Eagerness to get their hands on Dolly's money. Ruth, too, felt relief, but of a very different sort. For months, she had stockpiled her supplies of Ambien and Xanax, anticipating (and dreading) the day when she would administer a lethal dose to her mother. She saw herself smashing the pills to a fine powder, mixing them with vanilla ice cream and topping it with hot fudge and whipped cream. But as Dolly steadily declined, it was never quite the right time. And now that no less an authority than the Great Ziskin himself was calling the shots, Dolly's death would be in his hands, not Ruth's. It was almost as if Dolly had spared Ruth the burden, as she had done throughout her life. Don't bother making your bed, she would say, I'll do it. Don't bother with the dishes. Here, let me pay for that. Why poison me? Let the big shot doctor do it.

From the street, Saint Bernadette's Hospice looked like any other building. Nuns in contemporary dress drifted silently through the halls. Peach-colored rooms looked out to a courtyard with a well-tended garden. There was never anyone in the garden or in the Family Room which was furnished with a mouse-colored microsuede sofa and chairs, a play table for children and inspirational Christian books and magazines. Every day, the staff offered Ruth a hot lunch. She had no appetite. How could she eat roast chicken, mashed potatoes and peas while her mother was lying there on a diet of morphine and water?

"She can still hear," said a nurse. "You might want to play some of the CDs or just talk to her."

Dolly was as still as death. Eyes closed. Mouth open. If she can hear, I can fly, Ruth thought. Still, Ruth played the bland generic CDs provided by the hospice. Shit, she thought. Suppose the last thing Mom hears is *Dancing Queen* by Abba? She held her mother's limp hand, combed her hair and talked to her as a child converses with a doll, knowing that the doll will not respond. She watched the shallow rise and fall of Dolly's chest for hours on end. Sometimes Dolly groaned and Ruth rushed to find a nurse to increase the morphine. It was horrific enough to watch her mother die but she couldn't bare the thought of her mother regaining consciousness and being aware of what was happening.

Ruth sat in a reclining chair next to Dolly's bed all day and night. *I'm here, Mom, she said. I'll never leave you.* Miri came everyday without fail. Larry stopped by just long enough to cross-examine Ruth and the nurses. Naomi came and asked to be alone with Mother. Standing outside the door, Ruth saw Naomi take a prayer book from her bag, sit next to Dolly and read psalms. Shoshanna never made an appearance.

"Eat something," Miri said, nodding toward the half-dozen fruit baskets on the window sill. "You need your strength."

Ruth had no appetite but she gnawed on a pear to appease her aunt.

"Look at her," Miri said. "Still the prettiest girl in Brooklyn."

It was true. Even on her death bed, Dolly was beautiful. The morphine relaxed her face, erasing her wrinkles, bringing back the unlined brow and smooth cheeks of youth.

"Ever since her dementia started, I prayed for God to take her, to spare her the suffering. But now that it's happening, I'm not ready," Ruth said.

"It's never the right time to lose a mother," Miri said. "Come. Take a walk with me. There's something you need to know."

Please don't give me any more bad news, Ruth thought. If you've got cancer, heart disease or irritable bowel syndrome, I don't want to know about it. Not *now*. Miri led Ruth to the courtyard and lit up a cigarette. Bad sign. Miri had quit smoking years ago.

"Before your mother met your father, she had a boyfriend named Frank Martinelli," Miri said.

"Oh right, whenever she was mad at my father, she'd say I should've married my Italian boyfriend. But she never said why she didn't."

"She didn't marry Frank because, in those days, a nice Jewish girl didn't marry a Catholic. She was sixteen. He was nineteen. Frank was drafted and sent to Korea. Dolly promised to wait for him. But when he returned, she was already married to your father."

"I don't understand," Ruth said. "Why didn't she wait for Frank?"

"Because of me," Miri said.

"You? You were just a baby. How could you be responsible?"

"Do the math," Miri said. "I'm not your mother's sister, Ruth. I'm her daughter. Dolly and Frank's daughter. When her parent found out she was pregnant, they sent her to stay with cousins in Philadelphia. When she came back , they raised me as their own child."

"But if… if you're her daughter, you're my…"

"Sister. I'm your *sister*."

Ruth held onto the wooden bench as if it were a raft on the high seas. Everything she had believed to be true her entire life was shifting rapidly. Her docile, subservient mother had *another* life. A life that she could never fully forget because she saw her first love every time she looked into Miri's mischievous green eyes. But it was Ruth's own life that was in free fall. All those childhood Saturday afternoons when she had had Miri to herself, going to the Guggenheim, trying on hats at Saks, eating hot fudge sundaes at Rumplemeyer's, she had been with her *sister,* not her aunt. And all the many years she had blamed herself for not being able to break through Naomi's walls, Miri had been there. All along. Ruth threw herself into Miri's soft, brown arms.

"Oh, God. All these years," Ruth cried. "I always wanted a sister like you."

"You got me, kid. Always had. Always will."

Ruth wiped her eyes and blew her nose, trying to take it all in.

"Wasn't it difficult for you?" Ruth asked. "Having to pretend she wasn't your mother?"

"Actually, it was pretty good. I had two mothers who spoiled me rotten."

"What about your father, Frank? Did you ever see him?"

"Your grandparents didn't give him a chance to be involved. They pushed your mother into marriage before Frank came home from Korea. But I have this." Miri removed a gold locket from her neck and handed it to Ruth. Inside was photo of a darkly handsome boy in uniform.

"You look just like him," Ruth said. "Tell me, did my father know?"

"I'm sure he figured it out, but he never said anything. He adored your mother."

The story was sad. Yet thrilling. Dolly Sheraton had had a secret life, a passionate life, after all.

59

Oy, was it was hot! Dolly wanted to tear her clothes off. And what was that gurgling sound. The ocean? I must be at the beach, she thought. Where are the children? They've been in the water too long. Miri is supposed to be watching them but suppose she wandered off to talk to that lifeguard again? If I could just open my eyes. *LARRY! NAOMI! RUTHIE!* Dolly yelled but no sound came out.

With enormous effort, Dolly managed to open her eyes. Her lids felt like they were glued together. The light was blinding but she had to see. Sitting next to her in the shade of a red and white striped umbrella was a potato-faced woman in a black rayon dress, support hose rolled down below her lumpy knees.

"*Mammalla,*" Dolly gasped, using the Yiddish term of endearment for mother.

"*Shah Shah.* Go back to sleep," Bella said.

"But who's watching the children?"

"Don't worry. I've got my eye on them," her mother said, pointing an arthritic finger to a milky blue eye.

This made no sense. It took two strong adults to pull Bella out of a beach chair and she could no more run in the sand in her clunky orthopedic shoes than dance a mazurka. I'll just sleep for a few more minutes Dolly thought, then I'll take the children to the concession stand for Cherry Cokes. I'm so parched. Dolly fell back into a deep blue sleep, lulled by the crashing of the waves and the distant laughter of children.

60

"Why is she pulling at her nightgown?" Ruth asked.

"We don't know why they do that," said a nun, "But we see this a lot. We think that as they near the end, they want to be naked as when they were born."

Ruth bristled. Dolly was writhing, her face contorted.

"This is inhumane. Why can't you give her enough morphine to let her go?"

"Our job isn't to speed the dying process," the nun replied. "It's just to control pain."

Dogs are treated better than this, Ruth thought. Dolly had been on the IV drip for fourteen days. When another nun entered the room and started strumming a small harp, Ruth snapped.

"We're Jewish. I don't think my mother would appreciate that," she said.

Then again, if Dolly were to suddenly open her eyes and see a nun with a harp, she'd die from laughter. Not the worst option.

"Hearing is the last to go," the singing nun said.

"Yes, I know. I know," said Ruth. But she didn't buy it. Her mother had been comatose for two weeks.

"What kind of music does Mother like?"

Ruth thought. Her mother's taste ran to Perry Como, although she was also fond of the Beatles. She had wept when John Lennon was shot.

"Do you know *Let It Be*?" Ruth asked.

The nun nodded and strummed, singing in a high voice. Ruth joined in, humming more than singing. She didn't really believe her mother could hear but this seemed to placate the nun. What the hell.

"Look," said the nun.

Ruth looked. Dolly's eyes remained closed. Her body was immobile. But her dry, cracked lips moved. She was singing along. Soundlessly. But *singing.*

"She hears us. She hears us," Ruth cried, nervously wondering what she had said in her mother's presence these past weeks. *My god, I discussed her funeral plans and she heard every word!* For the next half hour, Ruth and the Singing Nun worked their way through the Beatles songbook and show tunes Dolly used to sing around the house. The nun improvised the melodies she didn't know, following Ruth's lead. When Ruth hummed Israel's national anthem *Hatikva* – because she didn't know the words – Dolly hummed along and smiled. Dolly had never visited Israel but every year she wrote a check to the Jewish Agency because "what they suffered, you should not know from."

When the nun tip-toed out of the room, Ruth put her lips near her mother's ear.

"Mom, promise me something. When you're on the other side, send me a signal, let me know you're okay."

* * * *

Witty came to the hospice with a box of over-priced chocolate coffee creams. They were Ruth's favorites but she just accepted them numbly and left them at the nurses' station. From time to time, a nurse would come in and peek under the sheet at the foot of the bed.

"What are you looking at?" Ruth asked.

"Lividity. When people are actively dying, their skin becomes mottled."

"Is she?"

"Not yet," The nurse lowered the sheet.

Ruth was tired from sleepless nights spent in a Barcolounger keeping watch over her mother. She had lost ten pounds and had raccoon eyes. When Miri arrived she insisted Ruth go home and rest.

"Go. Get out of here," she said. "Get some sleep. And, for God's sake, eat something."

Ruth went straight to Katya's. It was closer to the hospice than the El Coronado. She felt too tired to eat and too hungry to sleep.

"I'm just going to take a quick nap on your sofa," she told Katya,

As soon as she closed her eyes, Ruth plunged into a black pit of unconsciousness. Two hours later, Katya gently nudged her shoulder and whispered, "I'm leaving now. Stay as long as you like."

* * * *

"Dolly, wake up. Time to go."

"Five more minutes," Dolly said.

"No, *now*. Everybody's waiting."

With great effort Dolly sat up in her beach chair and opened her eyes. Again, the light was so bright she had to squint and shade her eyes with her hands. Her mother beckoned her to follow, trudging slowly across the burning sand.

"What about the chairs and umbrella?" Dolly asked.

"Leave them," Bella said.

In the distance, Dolly saw her parents 1959 Chevy Impala.

"Dad's car still works?" Dolly asked.

"Why shouldn't it work, with what we paid for it?"

A man waved from the driver's seat.

"C'mon already, traffic's gonna be murder," he shouted.

"Dad?" Dolly said. "DADDY?"

She hadn't seen her father in thirty years since he dropped dead while slicing corned beef for a customer. He had been bald at the time but now he had a thick crop of wiry black hair.

"Get in the back with Sol," he said.

Dolly peered into the back seat and there was Sol, lean and tan in a white linen shirt with his Bad Boy smile. She slid in beside him and kissed him on the mouth.

Bella climbed into the front passenger seat and her husband put the key in the ignition.

"Wait," cried Dolly. "The children! We can't leave without the children."

Bella turned around in her seat.

"Sweetheart, it's alright, the kids won't be joining us for a long time, god willing."

As the Chevy sailed along a wide, open highway towards a vast expansion bridge, Bella passed out salami sandwiches and Sol started to sing *"Off we go into the wild, blue yonder..."*

* * * *

Ruth sprang up from the sofa. She ran the six blocks to the hospice. People on the streets were shadows. *She knew.*

Miri stood by the door to Dolly's room.

"She waited until you were gone," Miri said.

They had removed the IV and tubes. Dolly was a wax figure, tucked tightly into fresh linens. Ruth placed her face against her mother's cheek and murmured into her angel soft hair. *Whither thou goes I shall go...*

61

"We'll get married. I'll take care of you." Witty said.

Staring over the precipice of her mother's grave and her own mortality, it seemed like a plan. Ruth would keep her own name. Ostensibly for professional reasons but, in actuality, to avoid being called Mrs. Hogworth. A nondenominational minister would officiate at the Ethical Society. For their honeymoon, they would go to St. Barts.

As to where they would live, Witty was magnanimous. Ruth could move into his penthouse. Or if she preferred, they would buy out her sibling's share of the apartment at the El Coronado.

"Whatever you think best, dear," he said.

Ruth was shopping for a wedding dress one week after she had thrown a shovel of dirt over her mother's coffin. Can brides wear black? Perhaps grey or blue, she thought. Yes, a mournful blue, the color of ominous, gathering clouds. I'm an orphan, she thought. An orphan who must marry a man of means.

* * * *

The Sheraton family was summoned to the law office of Finkle, Kaplow and Vontz for the reading of Dolly's will. Larry and Tory, Naomi and Howie, Ruth, Aunt Miri and assorted cousins marched somberly into the richly furnished conference room and seated themselves around the rosewood table. Shoshanna didn't attend. There were plastic Evian bottles, yellow legal pads and pens on the table and a large box of Kleenex. Jerry Finkle, the executor, sat at the head of the table, his three hundred pound girth spilling over the sides of an Eames chair.

"This is a sad day," he intoned. "Dolly was a wonderful woman and you, her family, were her *treasure*."

Tory, who was unfamiliar with the communal suffering that marks the loss of a Jewish mother, raised a brow and squeezed Larry's hand.

"I had the honor of drafting the changes in Dolly's wills over the years and, in each and every case, the language was clear. She wanted to be fair and show her love and devotion to you *all*."

Finkel took a moment to eyeball his audience.

"That being said, it has come to my attention that Dolly's most recent will, which was drawn up without my involvement, complies with the full requirements of the law and is to be upheld as follows."

Naomi chewed her lips. Larry's foot tapped so vigorously that Tory reached under the table to lay her hand on his knee. Ruth reached for a Kleenex. For her, the reading of the will was as wrenching as saying *kaddish*; it reaffirmed the unthinkable. Mommy was dead. Miri slid her chair closer to Ruth and rested a hand on Ruth's shuddering back. Finkel was droning on and on with legal mumbo jumbo when Larry's fist suddenly slammed the table so hard that Evian bottles rolled in every direction. Finkel stopped reading. He pushed his chair away from the table, preparing for the arduous task of rising to his full height of five feet.

"This is BULLSHIT," Larry yelled.

"Please," Finkel said, holding up one palm like a traffic cop. "Try and hold your responses until I have read the will in its entirety. I understand you have questions and I am here to answer them."

Ruth, who had tuned out the proceedings between the first "whereas" and the second "wherefore," leaned over and whispered to Miri, "What did I miss?"

"We're all cut out of the will," Miri said between gritted teeth.

"So who gets everything? Federation? Israel?"

Miri wrote on a name on a legal pad and passed it to Ruth. Ruth yelped, then quickly covered over her mouth. Meanwhile, Naomi was fidgeting with her cell phone and Howie was madly rubbing his face as if trying to erase his features. At the far end of the table, cousins grumbled amongst themselves. Finkle, who knew the situation was combustible and had seen, in this very room, his share of violence, pushed a button under the table. Seconds later, a young black lawyer entered.

"My colleague, Mr. Williams, will be sitting in with us," Finkle said.

Williams didn't have to do anymore than parade his massive shoulders for the room to quiet down.

"If I may continue," Finkle said.

No one said a word. They listened in rapt attention. The entire estate went to Shoshanna. The apartment. The jewelry. The Daum crystal. The cash. The stocks. The bonds. MILLIONS!

When Finkle finally opened the room to questions, Naomi raised her hand like one of her students.

"Yes?" Finkle said.

"I don't understand, Gerry," said Naomi. "How did this happen?"

"As I explained, Naomi, I assisted your mother in making revisions to her will over the years. However, according to the estate laws of New York, an attorney is not needed for a will to be valid. Naturally, I did a search to confirm that this was indeed your mother's Last Will and Testament."

"But, but it's just a piece of paper and mother wasn't well," Naomi sputtered.

"Actually, it's more than that. The execution of the will was videotaped, documenting that Dolly understood what she was signing and was in agreement at the time."

"Wait a minute. Wait just a goddamn minute," Naomi shouted. "I'm Shoshanna's mother. Are you telling me that my own daughter wrote me *out* of the will?"

"In a manner of speaking…."

"No, that can't be," Naomi whined. "That's not what Mother wanted. Larry, tell him. Tell him about the *other* will."

A vein bulged on Larry's forehead.

"SHUT UP YOU IMBECILE!" he yelled at Naomi.

"Don't talk to my wife that way," said Howie who was secretly thrilled to hear his brother-in-law give voice to what had been in his own heart for over twenty years.

"She's my sister," Larry growled. "I'll talk to her any fucking way I want, asshole."

Howie sprang out of his chair. So did Larry. They came towards each other, arms swinging, heads lowered.

"Gentlemen, please," Finkle cautioned.

"Larry, don't..." said Tory, fishing in her purse for her phone. If there was to be violence, she wanted it on video in case it ever went to court.

Howie and Larry both turned red in the face and insulted each other's manhood which was an unfair fight given Larry's auburn wig and Diane Von Fursentberg dress. A shoving match was in the works when Mr. Williams laid a heavy hand on Larry's shoulder. Larry turned and threw a wild punch that landed in Williams' gut, not hurting him as much as making him deeply unhappy. The cousins, three paunchy dress manufacturers with Rolex watches who had come more for entertainment than profit because they had already robbed Sol's side of the family blind, stood up and took off their jackets. It wasn't that they particularly liked Larry – the guy was a fruitcake – but he was *blood*.

62

"How long have you been feeling this way?" Dr. Ziskin asked.

"A few weeks."

She would've seen him sooner but, in the aftermath of her mother's death, it was all Ruth could do to get out of bed. At first, it just felt like a twenty-four hour bug. Upset stomach, headache, fatigue. But that was almost a month ago and it wasn't going away. If anything, she felt worse.

"Tell me if you feel any discomfort," he said, pressing her abdomen on the right side, the left and in the center. Ruth knew what he would find. She had gotten up at 2 a.m. the night before and researched her symptoms on the Internet. According to the Mayo Clinic, she most likely had a malignant tumor ripening in her womb or a dermoid cyst, a medical monstrosity with HAIR and TEETH. A chat room for insomniacs was no less comforting. Someone who called himself King Cobra told Ruth that aliens had set up shop in her body and the only way to release them was to take copious amounts of laxatives. Ziskin scribbled in Ruth's chart.

"Doctor, whatever it is, I want to know," she said.

"Of course, Dear. You've been through a lot lately," he said, putting his pen back into the chest pocket of his starched, monogrammed lab coat. "The loss of two parents in one year, it's no wonder you're having trouble sleeping and feeling anxious. I'd like to prescribe an anti-depressant. It will take two to three weeks to take effect...."

"I'm *not* depressed. Something's wrong with me physically," she said and, in doing so, confirmed the doctor's suspicions. Anxiety.

"I tell you what," said Ziskin, "To put you at ease, why don't I order a full panel blood test? Then we'll see where we go from there, okay?"

Maybe Ziskin was right. Her symptoms were probably nothing more than psychosomatic manifestations of bereavement. She had been weepy and having trouble sleeping since the funeral. Her appetite was erratic. One day, she couldn't eat a thing. The next, she gorged on moo shu pork. And God knows, 2 a.m. is not the hour to come to a conclusion about *anything*, let alone one's mortality. Ruth exchanged the baby blue paper dressing gown for the womb-like fleece hoodie and yoga pants she had been wearing (and sleeping in) for over a week. She turned her head as the nurse drew blood and got as far as the elevator, before running back to the doctor's office to throw up in the rest room. Rinsing her mouth, she looked in the mirror and thought about the signal she had asked her mother to send from the Great Beyond. Could this be it?

Walking down Madison Avenue, Ruth noticed how the dazzling shop windows had lost their allure. *These size two women with their permanently arched brows, walking with purpose, they are all going to DIE!* Okay, she thought, so maybe I am a wee bit depressed. She walked across Central Park from Fifth Avenue to the West Side, a distance she usually traversed by bus. A bus swept by sending up a gust of leaves. That's when Ruth knew what she had to do. She would write a blog about death. Not a morose thesis about terminal illness. No. She would write something wickedly funny about That Place From Which No One Returns.

Fueled by the rush that accompanies a new project, Ruth practically skipped to the apartment, got out her laptop and started making notes. Her father had expressed the belief that dying was like unplugging a TV. "When you're gone you're gone," he had said. But watching her mother lapse closer and closer to the edge, Ruth had the vague sense that there was a ghostly Cousins Club passing around kugel on the other side. She would research every belief system about the afterlife. Catholics, Baptists, Muslims, Buddhists, Seventh Day Adventists, Scientologists and Wiccans. She'd interview rabbis, priests, shamans, people who've been abducted by aliens. Rather than feeling depressed by the subject, Ruth was energized.

"A blog about *death*?" Gabby said glumly. "You know what happens when you talk about dying on television? People change the channel."

"It's not going to be morose. It'll be entertaining, edgy. I'll interview famous people – Ashton Kutcher, Lindsay Lohan, Jennifer Aniston - and ask what they think about the Hereafter."

"That's not a blog. That's a segment of *Access Hollywood*," quipped Gabby. "Look, Sweetums, there are better ways to cope with your mother's death than blogging. I mean, put it in your private journal if it makes you feel better, but not online where everyone can read it. It will *ruin* your career."

Ruth hadn't told Gabby about her visit to Ziskin. There would be time to share the details after she got the results of the blood test. If the news was bad? She envisioned herself lying in bed, wan and pale, in a beige lace peignoir. No, make that lavender. Waiting for her prescription for Lexapro at CVS, Ruth idly thumbed through *Cosmo*. While part of her brain absorbed "50 New Sex Moves to Drive Him Wild," another part gave serious consideration to her own funeral. This did not strike her as morbid. Not at all. She was merely planning ahead. She wanted to go out the way they do in New Orleans with mourners cake-walking to a Dixieland jazz ensemble. No doubt, a first for Mount Lebanon Cemetery.

"You look pale," Gabby said, "Why don't you take a nap in my tanning bed?"

"No, thanks," Ruth said. She was eager to go to La Perla to buy a peignoir – her wildly expensive shroud. She usually slept in a t-shirt and boxer shorts. But Death demanded a certain elegance and price was irrelevant. By the time the peignoir appeared on her credit card, Ruth reasoned she might be beyond the reach of debt collectors.

63

One week later, the anti-depressants had yet to kick in. Ruth felt as if she was slogging through Jello. Not the happy, quivering, whipped cream-topped dessert, but a viscous dun-colored gel that made every step an effort. It would've been easy to stay in bed all day but she forced herself to take a sentimental tour of her old neighborhood, from the El Coronado to 72nd Street and back again. She wore sunglasses to conceal her eyes which misted up at the most ordinary occurrence. Lovers at a sidewalk café, an old woman and her Scottie in matching red berets, a young woman pushing a stroller on a tree-lined street of elegant brownstones. It was all so crushingly *beautiful*.

She bantered with salesmen at Tip Top Shoes and ate a hot dog at Gray's Papaya. Her mother had always said you could die from eating hot dogs on the street. I'm dying anyway, Ma, we're *all* dying, Ruth thought as she topped her second dog with raw onions, relish and spicy mustard. She was seized by a craving to dine exclusively on street food. Samosas, tamales, tacos, pizza, Korean barbeque. I could write a blog about that too, she thought, ordering a second plate of cheese fries.

She marched up Broadway, bought a half dozen warm cinnamon raisin bagels and a bag of chocolate chip cookies at Zabar's. Ruth was gazing lustfully at the *schnecken* display when her cell phone rang.

"Ruth? This is Dr. Ziskin's office. Doctor would like you to come in to discuss your test results."

"But. But. He said he would *call* with the results."

"Yes, well, I'm calling to let you know Doctor would rather speak with you in person. How soon can you come in?"

The nurse's voice was pleasant as if scheduling an annual exam, not a death sentence, but that was her job, right? Don't scare the patients. Just get them in.

* * * *

Ziskin ushered Ruth into his study – the Bad News Room. This was where he had told the family about Dolly; now it was Ruth's turn. Ziskin folded his hands and looked over the top of his bifocals.

"Ruth, the tests have confirmed my suspicions."

"I'm dying," she said, burying her face in her hands.

"You're *not* dying," Ziskin said. "You're pregnant. Mazel Tov."

Ruth looked at him from between her fingers.

"I *can't* be pregnant," she said.

Ziskin was used to hearing this kind of denial from naïve teenagers but not from a woman old enough to know better.

"What have you been using for birth control?" he asked.

"Spanx." It was a joke that always got a laugh. Not here.

"I beg your pardon?" said Ziskin.

"I haven't been using anything because I didn't think... I didn't think it was possible."

"You still get normal periods, don't you?"

"Yes but…"

Ziskin rattled on, detailing the tests recommended for pregnant women over forty. Ruth had zoned out. *How did this happen??* Technically, she knew. She had been having sex with two men right up until… *OH MY GOD! Whose baby is it?*

"How far along am I?" she asked, interrupting the doctor's train of thought.

"Three months. That accounts for your nausea which normally dissipates around this time. The pressure on your bladder, however…"

Ruth tuned out again. How would she break the news to Witty?

"Ruth. RUTH." Ziskin said.

"Sorry, I was just thinking…" she said, unaware that her right hand had been caressing her belly the entire time.

"Well, you have a lot to think about. I'd like to refer you to a specialist in mature pregnancies." Worry creased Zizkin's brow. "Unless, of course, you don't want to go through with it?"

"Yes. No. I mean, I don't know."

Ruth left the office with a brochure *You're Expecting!* and the address of an abortion clinic. If she had written this for a sit-com, the idea would've been shot down with much rolling of eyeballs. A middle-aged woman with two lovers gets pregnant? Yada yada yada. But this was no TV series. It was her life. The only approval needed to "green light" the project growing in her belly was her own.

64

After a fundraising dinner for a Gluten Free Society, Ruth broke the news to Witty in a Starbucks.

"That's marvelous, dear," he gushed. "I'm thrilled. Positively thrilled."

This wasn't what Ruth expected. Or more to the point, it wasn't the script she had been rehearsing all day.

"There are other things you should know," she said, stirring her decaf latte,"The baby might not be yours." *There. I said it.* She stiffened waiting for shock to sink in.

"I must say I'm disappointed, Ruth," his voice was barely a whisper. "But I am deeply moved by your honesty. This couldn't have been easy for you."

Holy crap. Now what?

"I forgive you," he said in the neutral tone of a priest dispensing absolution. "Nothing destroys a relationship like lies and deception. At least we are starting off with a clean deck."

"As long as we're clearing the air, there are other things you should know," she said. "I'm not thirty-nine. I'm forty-two," she said.

"No!" he gasped playfully, "A woman lying about her age? What next?"

"About my mother's condo…," she said.

"Sweetheart, I told you. We'll do whatever you desire. Live there. Sell it. Rent it out. Whatever."

"That's no longer option," she said.

"Oh? Why not?"

"I was disinherited. The entire estate is going my niece Shoshanna."

Witty leaned back and blinked his eyes rapidly as if trying to get Ruth into focus. *Thank God. I finally hit a nerve.*

"That's unconscionable," he said. "You have to fight this. Hire a lawyer."

"I've been over it with an attorney. It's uncontestable. Even my brother has given up."

"But how....?"

"I think it's some kind of poetic justice." Ruth said with a rueful smile. "Shoshanna was the only grandchild. That gave her a certain immunity to our squabbles."

"But, from what I've gathered, she's a very manipulative, narcissistic creature. You told me yourself. Shoshanna never showed any interest in your mother until she was seriously ill."

"Well, what does it matter now?" Ruth said, blithely tossing her napkin on the table. "It's only money. That's what my father used to say. 'Sweetheart, it's only money'."

Witty looked horrified. He started to fidget. He cracked his knuckles, did odd things with his neck as if trying to unscrew his head. When he finally spoke, his voice came from far away.

"The hell with the wedding plans," he said, taking her hand. "Let's get married immediately. Tomorrow, if you want."

Ruth had only one more bullet. She let it fly.

"I can't marry you," she said twisting off her ring and placing on the table. "I don't love you."

Witty stared at the ring, at Ruth, and back at the ring.

"Darling, you're pregnant. Your hormones are raging. You don't know what you're doing."

"You're right," she said. "I don't know what I'm doing. But whatever it is, I'm going to do it on my own."

65

"You should've kept the ring," Gabby said.

It was two p.m. Gabby was enthroned in her Louis IV bed, propped up with dozens of tasseled cushions, having her third or fourth drink of the day. Who's counting? Certainly not Gabby. Light filtered through the silk drapes. As always, she wore full stage makeup with a double set of false eyelashes, a glossy apricot wig and a pink marabou-trimmed bed jacket.

"I'm pregnant," Ruth said.

"You're *WHAT?*" Gabby's head whirled around so fast her wig slipped over one eye.

"Pregnant."

"At *your* age?"

Why do people always say that? I'm forty-two, not fifty-two.

"Is Mr. Moneybags the father?" Gabby asked.

"Maybe. Maybe not."

"What are you gonna do?" said Gabby, addressing her question to Ruth's stomach.

"Haven't decided."

Gabby refilled her glass with Moet Chandon and slurped it noisily.

"Look. I don't want you worrying about money," Gabby said. "Now that your fiancé isn't picking up the tab, I'll put you on a retainer. An extra five hundred a week. Just keep your receipts."

"That's very generous but it won't be enough for me to stay in Manhattan now that I have to vacate my parent's condo," Ruth said, climbing off the bed, moving toward the window.

"Vacate? Why?"

"It's a long story involving lawyers, guns and money. Well, two out of three."

Gabby threw back her Pierre Deux bed linens and jumped out of bed. "You're *leaving* me?"

Below her frou frou bed jacket, Gabby wore pink nylon underpants which exposed puffy white thighs. Ruth turned away, pretending to be fascinated by the traffic on East 75th Street.

"You're having a meltdown, Ruth," Gabby said. "You lost your mother. Found out your Fuck Monkey was fucking around. Now you're knocked up. Well, I won't hear of it. You're not going *anywhere*."

It was difficult to read the emotions flickering across Gabby's Botoxed face. She wrapped her marabou-covered arms around Ruth and squeezed hard.

"But I really can't stay in Manhattan," Ruth said, "LA is more affordable and I still have contacts in the biz and a support network."

Half a dozen gay friends, a bungalow in Silver Lake and a job writing Saturday morning cartoons. It could be worse.

"Nonsense. I'm getting too old to host a morning show. I want to produce and I want you to be my head writer."

"A talk show or sitcom?" Ruth asked.

"How the fuck should I know? We'll talk. We'll figure it out."

Ruth's right hand drifted to her stomach protectively.

"I'm flattered, Gabby, but I can't just wing it anymore. I need stability in my life."

"Stability, huh?" Gabby grabbed her Iphone, squinted at it and punched in a number. "Ben? Gabby. Draw up a contract for Ruth Sheraton, my new head writer..." She turned to Ruth, "He wants to know how much?"

Ruth opened and closed her mouth like a blow fish.

"Make it in the low six figures for now," Gabby growled. "We'll work out the details later."

"God, Gabby, I didn't expect this. I don't know what to say."

"I can see that. You're not a planner," Gabby said to Ruth's stomach. "Now get the hell outta here and find yourself a decent apartment."

66

The realtor tried to push Ruth into a hi-rise condo with a lap pool just off Park Avenue. She resisted and took an apartment in a pre-war building on Riverside, walking distance to the 79th Street boat basin. What cinched the deal was the bay window seat and river view. Ruth furnished it with mid-century furniture she found at the Chelsea Flea Market, including a set of chartreuse Russell Wright dishes that looked exactly like the ones she had reluctantly parted with when she left LA, right down to a slight chip on the lip of a pitcher. The big splurge was a dark chocolate Roset Lignet sofa. She placed a silver-framed photograph of her parents at Sardis, circa 1959, on the mantel.

Ruth started each day with an early morning walk along the marina, then Zabar's for a warm cinnamon raisin bagel with a schmear and a decaf latte. Back at her apartment, she sat in her window seat and worked on the sitcom pilot script, from time to time, staring out at boats bobbing in the Marina. Gabby wanted the show to be about women over forty balancing careers and relationships in the city.

"But edgy. I want to make the censors sweat," said Gabby.

"What about bigamy?" Ruth asked. Enough time had gone by that her bogus marriage was ripe for satire.

"Mormans?" Gabby smirked.

"No. Not *polygamy*. Just a regular, bright, career woman in New York who finds out her husband has another family. Maybe in Queens?"

"Funny. But can you make it believable?"

Can I ever, Ruth thought. She had toyed with a character based on Witty, a dapper parolee, but had second thoughts when she spotted a news item in the Style Section of the *New York Times.* "Katya Romanov-Schmuckler and Dewitt Clinton Hogworth announce their engagement…"

Poor Dr. Schmuckler, Ruth thought. Then again, a divorced Manhattan plastic surgeon will not be lonely for long. She took the high road and sent Witty and Katya a crystal bowl from Tiffany's. Filled with mixed nuts. She selected a more practical item for her brother's engagement. Matching monogrammed bathrobes. Larry still had his jagged edges but Tory was filing them down.

Miri was thrilled with Ruth's new apartment and career advancement. Even Shoshanna expressed enthusiasm. Apparently, she had soured on the idea of living at the El Coronado. Something about the refrigerator door opening at odd hours and the sound of an old Jewish couple bickering. She quickly unloaded the condo and was using the proceeds to launch her career in reality television.

"I want to be just like you," Shoshanna told Ruth. "But richer."

Occasionally, Ruth received postcards from faraway places with inadequate plumbing, signed *Peace and love, Naiomi.* And, once, on a Friday evening stroll up Broadway Ruth saw Howie walking arm-in-arm with the woman he had been with at MoMA. But he didn't say hello. He rubbed his eye furiously and ran in the opposite direction.

Ruth's favorite part of the day was late afternoon. When she couldn't write another snippet of dialogue and the sun was low, slicing the river into golden sheets of light, she walked to a small park along the boat basin.

"Do you mind?" asked a young woman, sitting next to Ruth on a park bench, whipping out a breast and attaching a squirming infant to her nipple.

"Not at all," Ruth replied.

"Which one is yours?" the breast-feeding woman asked, looking towards children happily playing in puddles and dirt.

"This one," Ruth said, patting her stomach.

This one.

The End

www.ingramcontent.com/pod-product-compliance
Lightning Source LLC
Chambersburg PA
CBHW070904180626
46817CB00003B/911